“You could have worn…something.” Lucy heard the nervous edge to her voice with dismay and took a few deep, steadying breaths.

“I could have,” he admitted.

“Then why didn’t you?”

Nick propped himself up on his side, resting on an elbow, with the sheets draped haphazardly over his lower body.

“Because I wanted to make love to you,” he replied.

“You…what?” A warm, sweet sensation filled her body.

“Don’t tell me that you haven’t guessed by now that I am attracted to you.”

“But we’re here on business!” She clung to that scrap of truth with tenacity. “And… you’re my boss!”

“That didn’t stop us once before….”

**They're the men who have everything—
except a bride...**

Wealth, power, charm—
what else could a handsome tycoon need?
In THE GREEK TYCOONS miniseries you
have already been introduced to some
gorgeous Greek multimillionaires who are
in need of wives.

Now it's the turn of talented
Presents® author Cathy Williams,
with her sparkling intense office romance
Constantinou's Mistress.

This tycoon has met his match, and he's decided
he *has* to have her...*whatever* that takes!

Look for the next title in this series
The Greek's Secret Passion
by
Sharon Kendrick

On sale in September, #2345

Only in Harlequin Presents!

Cathy Williams

CONSTANTINOU'S MISTRESS

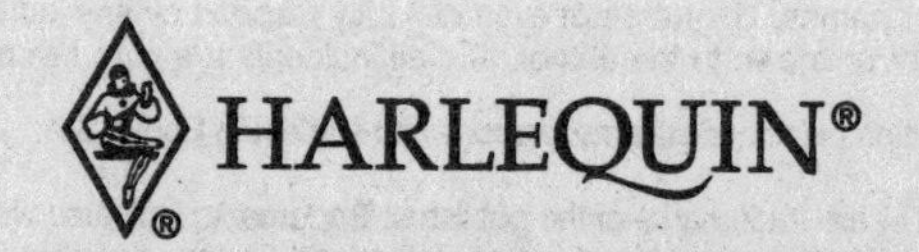

TORONTO • NEW YORK • LONDON
AMSTERDAM • PARIS • SYDNEY • HAMBURG
STOCKHOLM • ATHENS • TOKYO • MILAN • MADRID
PRAGUE • WARSAW • BUDAPEST • AUCKLAND

ISBN 0-373-12340-X

CONSTANTINOU'S MISTRESS

First North American Publication 2003.

This edition published by arrangement with Harlequin Books S.A.

Visit us at www.eHarlequin.com

Printed in U.S.A.

CHAPTER ONE

LUCY heard the distant thud of a door slamming shut and her hand stilled over the computer keyboard.

There shouldn't be anyone in the place. Not at this time of the night, almost ten-thirty, and certainly not on this day of all days. She slowly pushed back the chair, feeling horribly vulnerable in the brightly lit room, the only lit room in the entire building. Anyone could be approaching, looking in at her, and she wouldn't be able to see a thing.

Imposing as Nick Constantinou's office was, there was nowhere to hide. No convenient empty cupboards or, for that matter, thick velvet curtains. The windows, on the second floor of the smoked-glass building, were bare of handy thick curtains and somehow trying to slip her frame, slight though it was, behind the pale wooden shutters would have been ludicrous.

In fact, the whole idea of hiding was ludicrous. Lucy Reid was far too sensible a person to entertain thoughts of robbers and muggers.

She cleared her throat and briskly made her way to the thick door that connected Nick Constantinou's office to her own. Then she tiptoed into the enveloping darkness of her own office and peered tentatively out of the door, not expecting to see anything at all. The high, wintry winds gusting outside had a nasty habit of rattling leaves against window-panes, and when everywhere was wrapped in silence the sound of leaves against a window-pane was like the crash of a boulder through glass.

So her heart leapt to her throat when a dark figure lurched from one of the adjoining offices back out into the corridor and straight in her direction.

'Yes? May I help you?' *May I help you? At ten-thirty in the evening in an office building which she had made sure to lock behind her when she had come in two hours previously?* The inadequacy of her high-pitched question brought a gurgle of sick, nervous laughter to her throat.

'Who are you?' Lucy pressed herself back against the wall and wondered how fast her feet would be able to carry her should she need to make a bolt for the staircase. She was only five feet three and the figure bearing down towards her looked at least a foot taller and broad with it.

'Who do you think I am?' The figure reached out to bang on a switch on the wall and suddenly the corridor was flooded with light and she released a sigh of shuddering, heartfelt relief. 'A wild, dangerous bandit out to plunder the very—' he waved one arm in a sweeping gesture '—luxurious offices of Constantinou Enterprises?' He seemed to find his own rhetorical question insanely funny because he suddenly laughed, flinging his head back and leaning against the wall for support while Lucy watched in consternation.

'What are you doing here, Nick?' She walked hesitantly towards the towering figure. 'Shouldn't you be…? Are you all right?'

'Shouldn't I be…where?' The laughter had stopped as abruptly as it had begun, and as he stared at her she could see the dark shadows under his eyes and the distinctly bleary look of someone under the influence of alcohol.

It was shocking enough to almost halt her in her tracks. Nick Constantinou didn't drink. Or at least she had never seen him drink, not at a single one of any of the social occasions which she had attended with him over the past ten months, in her capacity as secretary.

'You haven't answered my question!'

'Question? What question?' Lucy stammered.

'Where do you think I should be?' He strolled towards her very carefully. Even drunk, as he undoubtedly was, Nick Constantinou still emanated a fierce, unstudied masculine power that could take her breath away. The sombreness of his clothing, black trousers, black tie, loosened and revealing a sliver of hard, bronzed chest, big black coat that swayed around him like a dangerous magician's cloak, only served to emphasise his innate aggression. His dark hair was tousled from the wind outside and he raked his fingers restlessly through it.

'I thought you might be...well, have stayed behind at your house with all your relatives...' After all, the funeral of his late wife had taken place earlier in the day.

'I need to sit down.' He brushed past her down towards his office and disappeared through the door, leaving her to wage a frantic internal debate as to whether she should follow him or else leave the premises as quickly and quietly as she could.

The choice was removed from her when she heard him bellow from the bowels of his office, 'Bring me some water, Lucy! Or, better still, a cup of black coffee!'

'Water would be better.' She groped her way through the office, which was now in darkness, and switched on the light on his desk. 'If you've drunk a lot, then you'll be dehydrated. You need to drink as much water as you can.'

'Always sensible, are you not?' he mocked, taking the glass from her and propping himself up on the massive sofa that consumed a good part of one wall. 'Always dependable when it comes to good, sound advice.'

Lucy winced. Yes, good old dependable Lucy, who had climbed up through the ranks of Constantinou's head office through a combination of hard work, supreme efficiency and an ability not to lose her head, whatever the provocation. Good old Lucy, who couldn't be in the same room as her boss without feeling a flutter of awareness, whose eyes were fond of lingering on his harsh profile when she knew he wasn't watching, whose mind ached with images of him, not only forbidden fruit because he was married, but also utterly beyond the reach of someone as ordinary as she was.

'So you think I should be safely back at my own home, do you?' Nick lay back on the sofa with his arm slung over his eyes and his hand resting lightly around the glass on his flat, hard stomach.

Yes, he thought to himself, he should be back at the house, grieving in his widower's garb and allowing relatives, some of whom he had never laid eyes on, to pour their heartfelt sympathy on his head.

The thought of it brought a wave of nausea rushing up his throat.

'Does anyone know where you are? Perhaps I should call…'

'No!' He whipped his arm away and looked at her with brilliant black eyes. 'I do not need to be rescued like an invalid who is no longer in charge of his own behaviour!'

'They might be worried,' Lucy persisted, hovering indecisively over him.

'Sit. My neck is beginning to ache looking up at you.'

She moved to pull one of the chairs across and he said

irritably, 'Just perch on the edge of the sofa. You will be perfectly safe, I assure you.'

'Well...if you want to be alone, you know, perhaps the best thing would be for me to go...'

'What are you doing here anyway?' Nick asked, ignoring her suggestion. 'Skulking in an office at eleven in the night? Have you nowhere else to go?'

'Of course I do!' Lucy's temper snapped and she glared at him from under her lashes. 'I just felt a little...restless, if you want to know. Funerals...' the single word dropped into the silence between them like a stone, and she cleared her throat awkwardly before continuing '...depress and unsettle me. I thought I might be able to lose myself if I came here and caught up on some work. I know it seems a little odd, but...' Her hands fidgeted on her lap and she was holding herself so rigid that she could feel every muscle in her slender body aching from the tension.

'Funerals are depressing,' Nick said in a flat, expressionless voice.

'Nick, I know I said this to you today, but I really am...very, very sorry. I don't know...would it help to talk about what happened?'

'What happened was a car crash.' He pressed his thumbs over his eyes and felt another sharp stab of guilt that the emotion most expected of him—sorrow—was so patently absent.

Gina had, outwardly, been everything a man could ever want, beautiful, sexy and exotically enticing, with a habit of flicking her long black hair and narrowing her eyes that could make a man do the unforgivable.

And for a very short while he had been as enamoured of her as any other man would have been, enamoured enough to walk up the aisle, confident that what he felt would last for eternity.

But it hadn't lasted. He could truthfully say that his two years of marriage could be reduced to four months of happiness and then a long process of facing the inevitable.

'How much have you had to drink?'

'Enough to try and forget.'

'She was very beautiful,' Lucy said gently. 'I can't imagine what a nightmare these past two weeks must have been for you…'

'Then I suggest you do not bother to try,' Nick told her abruptly. His body was beginning to feel like a dead weight and his thoughts were blurred. Her voice was like a soothing flow of water around him. For one wild moment he actually hovered on the brink of telling her the truth, that the nightmare of grief she imagined him to be going through was a different sort of nightmare.

It was a nightmare of remembering the months of witnessing his wife's unruly behaviour, her vicious accusations that he wasn't man enough to satisfy her, that the only true lover in his life was his work. Every accusation had removed him further and further away from any lingering affection he might have felt towards her, and when her evenings out had begun to stretch into the odd night away he had reached a point of indifference.

But still he had held on, powerless to take the final step to terminate their marriage. When the call had come from her father in Greece that she had been involved in a car crash, speeding along one of the narrow, perilous roads that wound their way out of the city towards the family retreat in the hills, he had gone immediately, braced for some sort of remorse that if he had just paid her a bit more attention then she might not have stormed out of their London flat to have a bit of fun somewhere else.

The remorse had never come. The car crash had told its own sordid story of adultery, with her lover's body in the passenger seat next to her, holding her in a final, mortal embrace.

He blearily wondered what his reliable, efficient secretary would say to such revelations and gave a wry, bitter grimace. Lucy was not a woman of the world. He opened his eyes and looked at her in frank appraisal, until he noticed her pale skin beginning to redden under the inspection.

'You blush like a teenager,' he said thickly. 'I must have scared the hell out of you when you saw me in the corridor.' His mind cleared a bit to accommodate that thought and he actually grinned with genuine amusement. 'I am surprised you did not lock yourself in the office and call the police.'

'It did occur to me,' Lucy admitted with a reluctant smile. 'You were the last person I was expecting to see.'

'The atmosphere in the house was getting to me. The funeral was…bad enough, but being surrounded by two Greek communities, both sides wondering why she was being buried over here…tearful, sympathetic smiles barely hiding their thoughts that, as a Greek, she should have been buried over there…too much…had to get away…'

It was more than he would ever have confessed had he been sober. In fact, he wondered whether he would have confessed as much to anyone else. Probably not. But Lucy sat there, looking at him with such soft compassion that he found himself unable to resist the urge to confide at least some of what was going through his head. Madness.

'Why *did* you choose to have her…you know…buried over here?'

'This is where she lived and it is where I live. It was appropriate.' His mouth twisted in a mimicry of a smile. 'After all, should I not have a memory close by me of my beloved wife?' A constant reminder, he thought bitterly, of the emptiness of the institution of marriage and the treachery of the female sex.

Lucy nodded and lapsed into silence.

Eventually, she cleared her throat. 'I think it's time I left now. Will you be all right here on your own? Are you sure you wouldn't like me to call someone to come and be here with you? At times like this…you might find company helpful…'

'I have company already.'

The dark, heavy-lidded eyes broodingly roamed over her face until she could feel every nerve-ending in her body tingle.

This was a first, to have his eyes settle on her and know that what he was seeing wasn't his highly capable and utterly sexless secretary, and she could hear the clang of alarm bells ringing in her head.

The man had had too much to drink, was in the throes of a grief her mind could only begin to comprehend, and as such was in control of nothing, not even his thoughts. She had no idea what he was seeing when he looked at her the way he was looking at her now, with unblinkered concentration. It certainly wasn't *her*. Maybe he was seeing the face of his wife, although how that could be was beyond her. Physically she was as different from Gina as chalk from cheese. Petite, boyishly slim with pale skin and short fair hair as opposed to voluptuously sexy, dark-eyed, olive-skinned with long black hair.

But she had dreamt of him for so long, had conjured

up so many feverish images of being touched by him, that it was wickedly, pathetically, disturbingly exciting to have his attention focused on her.

'It's getting late, Nick; I really should be going...'

'Or else what?'

'I beg your pardon?'

'Or else what? Is anyone expecting *you* back at your house?'

'Well...'

'Your parents?'

'I don't live with my parents! My parents live in Cornwall!' How *old* did he think she was? Twelve?

'My unreserved apologies.' He gave her a slow, lazy smile that sent the blood rushing through her body. 'You look horrified that I could imply such a thing.' There was something else in his expression now, something she couldn't quite put her finger on; she just knew that, whatever it was, it was wreaking havoc with her already frazzled sense of composure. 'You're still in your funeral garb,' he pointed out. 'How long have you been here? Beavering away?'

'I...I didn't go back to your house after the service. I'm sorry. I couldn't face...'

'Hordes of sympathisers? Seems almost obscene to have so many people gathered together at such a time, does it not? Chatting, catching up on old times with relatives they have not laid eyes on for years, making sure to keep their expressions suitably mournful.'

The cynicism in his voice made her flinch and she reminded herself that grief worked in different ways. Not everyone wore their feelings on their sleeve and Nick Constantinou would never be one of those who bared their soul and wept in front of an audience. That didn't mean that his grief was any less profound.

'It's a difficult time,' Lucy said evasively. 'Look…'

'Don't go.' He reached out and captured her wrist in his hand and a searing heat flooded her body. 'Not yet.'

'Would you like another glass of water?' she said desperately. Her hand lay passively in his grip but she was acutely and painfully aware of the pressure of his palm against her flesh. 'You should drink as much water as you can,' she babbled on helplessly while her eyes fluttered with nervous fascination across his dark, shadowed face.

'Stay. Talk to me. Tell me what you did after you left the church. Where did you go?'

'I…well, I went to the supermarket. I meant to get back home but the supermarket was packed and it took me much longer than I thought to get around it. Almost an hour and a half! This is so dreary, so dull…'

'I find your voice soothing.'

'Right…' Now he was absent-mindedly stroking the inside of her wrist with his thumb and sending hundreds of electric currents running up and down her arm. She could feel her brain struggling to impose order on what was happening but his black eyes were mesmerising. 'Well…' She gave a high-pitched, unsteady little laugh. 'If you really want to know, I left the supermarket, dropped the stuff off at my flat and then decided that I couldn't face staying there, so I drove to a restaurant and had something to eat…'

'On your own?'

'On my own.'

'I thought women never went to restaurants on their own. Gina would never have dreamt of doing that.' He gave a short, hard laugh. Oh, no, Gina would never have done that, not in a month of Sundays. She had never cared for her own company. She had always needed an audience, preferably of the male variety, someone for whom she could toss her hair and flash her eyes, someone to lean across to, making sure that her bountiful breasts hinted at pleasures only she could dispense.

'Well, it doesn't bother me,' Lucy said with an edge of defensiveness in her voice. 'I know you probably think that's very sad, a woman of twenty-three eating in a restaurant on her own on a Friday night, but I've never been the sort who needs constant companionship.' It occurred to her that the mere fact that she felt compelled to defend herself made her sound sad. She didn't sound at all like the liberated young thing she wanted to show him that she was.

'I don't think it is sad at all.'

'Anyway, I should have gone back home after that but I fancied a drive. I don't often get the chance. I take the tube in to work and tonight I thought I'd drive and I ended up driving here. At the time it seemed a good idea to come in and finish off some work. I don't know why. I don't know what I was thinking. I just wasn't very tired.'

'I am very glad you weren't.' He released her wrist but only to trail one long finger along her arm.

What was going on? Nick didn't know. He looked at her and his body started to react. A tense silence closed around them and he felt as though time had carried them away to a little world where reality was something that no longer existed.

All that existed were his confused thoughts and this woman sitting alongside him on a sofa in his office. And he wanted her there, a warm, living, breathing person.

She had dressed in suitably sober clothing for the funeral. A dark skirt, a deep-burgundy long-sleeved top. Her jacket and coat she had discarded. He had noticed her at the funeral and the black coat had swathed her and made her look like a fragile waif with those huge brown eyes and small, delicate face. Small, delicate face with a perfectly shaped mouth, one he now found himself touching with the tips of his fingers.

Lucy gripped his fingers with one shaky hand and lowered them to her lap. She had to get out of there and very quickly. 'Look, I know you've just been through the most awful experience you may ever have to go through in your life, but…what you need is sleep, Nick.'

'No, that is not what I need,' he murmured back, drowsily running his eyes over her face and then along her body. She always dressed for work smartly, in suits with crisp shirts underneath boxy jackets. Never before had he felt himself yearning to touch what was so purposefully concealed, but then, he thought to himself, he had always been a married man. Married to the notion of fidelity, too damned stubborn and proud to admit failure even when their ship had been sinking and he'd been able to feel his feet wavering unsteadily on their collapsing foundations.

Now, though…the burgundy top which clung to Lucy's small frame compelled him to look at the swell of her breasts, and he could see by the way she was breathing that what he was doing was turning her on. He was sure of it. She dropped his hand and clasped her arms across her chest. Didn't she know that that gesture only aroused his imagination, made him want to prise those arms away and touch what she was protecting?

Lord, he must be going mad!

He passed his hand over his brow and then raked his fingers through his hair.

'Have *you* ever thought about getting married?' he asked.

Lucy, caught unawares, stared at him for a few silent seconds. 'Of course. Don't all women? Dream of settling down and living happily ever after with Mr Right?' Stop talking, she told herself fiercely. Just get a grip and leave! But her feet were blocks of lead.

'Happily ever after?' His laugh was brutally cynical. 'Let me know what that feels like if you ever find it.'

He sure as hell hadn't. He had barely found the happy bit, never mind the ever after.

Lucy, watching the harsh twist of his mouth, felt a rush of sympathy for the man lying on the sofa. The ruthlessly self-assured boss she had spent months working for, the man who could walk into any crowded room and reduce the occupants to silence simply by his sheer presence, was strangely and touchingly defenceless now.

His cynicism was so understandable. For him, there would be no fairy-tale ending to his fairy-tale marriage.

Impulsively, Lucy reached out and took one of his big hands in hers.

He pushed himself further up the sofa so that he was now semi-sitting, his head resting against the wood-panelled wall behind him.

'God, I feel as though I've run a marathon uphill all the way.'

'You must be exhausted,' she agreed. 'You look it.' Then she did the unthinkable, did it without even stopping to think. She reached out and traced her finger across one of his hard cheekbones.

Nothing, to Nick, had ever felt sweeter. Could that finger taste as sweet as it had felt just then? He softly held it and closed his eyes, circling it with his lips. Then he was kissing all her fingertips, his eyes still closed. The humming that had been going on in his head ever since he had started on the whisky hours earlier had disappeared, replaced by a different sort of noise. The roll of thunder.

He pulled her towards him, holding his hand behind the nape of her neck, and blindly sought her mouth. His lips met hers with a heat that drove the breath out of his throat and he framed her face with both his hands, pulling her towards him.

'Nick...you don't need this...' The utterance made her see clearly what she didn't want to see. That, although *he* might not need it, *she* did. Against every thread of ingrained common sense, the utter foolishness of the feelings she had been harbouring towards him for months pushed their way through to seize control of her mind.

'I need...' What *did* he need? Solace? Forgetfulness? Another chance to live the past two years all over again without repeating the mistakes that had hardened his soul? 'I need comfort,' he heard himself say, and this time when their mouths met it was with gentleness. He ran his tongue over her lips and then inside, feeling the mingle of moisture that tasted of honey.

This is madness, Lucy thought. He wasn't thinking straight. He wasn't even thinking. He said he wanted comfort and comfort from any source would do the trick—and not even comfort of the kind her body was compelling her to give him.

'You need to get some sleep,' she muttered into his mouth. 'Why don't you let me drop...drop you home...?'

Nick didn't answer. He pulled her until she was half lying on him and ran his fingers through her short hair.

'Did you ever have long hair?' he murmured, his eyes half-closed. 'I can't imagine you with long hair somehow.'

'I have to go.'

'Short hair suits you.' His hand slipped beneath the stretchy top and her breath caught in her throat. She made an unsteady effort to push herself away but every nerve in her body was burning with a wild, suffocating need. It was as if her feelings had been locked away in a bottle and now the lid had been taken off and every pent-up drop of forbidden yearning was sweeping out in a frenzy of abandonment.

'Like a gazelle,' he said huskily, bringing his hand up until it covered one of her small, perfectly formed breasts.

Lucy gave a little squeak of shock and he pushed his fingers into the lacy bra so that he could feel the sensitive bud of a nipple.

'No, we can't do this…'

'I need you, Lucy, to make me warm…'

'No, you don't.'

'Let me see you.'

'Nick…'

'Take off the jumper. Let me see you.'

Her senses were swimming in confusion but she couldn't tear her fixated eyes away from his face. With a soft shudder of horrified compulsion that was mingled with searing compassion, she felt herself slowly work the jumper up and over her head until she was leaning over him with only her bra on, nothing to hide the rapid rise and fall of her chest. Her erratic breathing matched his and with a groan he pulled down the straps of her bra. Small, dainty breasts pointed up at him with their big, rosy peaks. Breasts that were sweetly aroused. He could tell by the tight, hard bud crowning the centre of the perfectly defined pink discs. Her mouth was half-parted in fascination and the urge to lose himself in the slim, flawless body nervously displaying itself for his greedy gaze was overpowering.

He dipped his head and bent forward and began to suckle at the nipple, only vaguely aware of her own hiss of indrawn breath and the satisfied arching of her body. Then her hands curled into his hair and she cupped his face while he continued to suck the extended tip of her nipple, only breaking off to smother the breast with wet kisses before moving on to explore the splendid feast of the other.

His erection was almost painful, and as he continued to give her breast his undivided attention he guided her hand to his trousers, keeping it there while he fumbled with his zipper.

This couldn't be happening! Watching him, feeling him, as he nuzzled against her breasts, nipped and sucked at her nipples, was mind-blowing enough, but as her hands closed snugly around his swollen shaft she felt a ripple of uncontrollable need rush through her.

She pulled back, but only so that she could stand up and wriggle feverishly out of her cloying skirt and out of the tights and underwear that she barely had the patience to rid herself of.

She needed to feel his hard body alongside hers on the sofa but he was not having it, not yet. He cupped the bare flesh of her bottom with his hands and pulled her towards him so that he could blow softly on the soft, fine triangle of hair that led down to the crease of her closed thighs.

Lucy released a shuddering moan and flung her head back, parting her legs as he began to explore her most intimate region, flicking into folds of her womanhood, turning her into a raging flame.

She gripped the back of his head with unsteady hands and rotated her hips slightly against him. When she was on the brink of exploding he pulled back and yanked her down on top of him. She felt the thrust of him against her own throbbing arousal and the smooth fabric of his trousers against her legs.

There was something headily sensual about the fact that she was totally naked while he still had on his shirt, rumpled though it was, and his trousers. She felt a thrilling, unexpected surge of power and climbed onto him, eyes open wide so that she could see the sheer beauty of his face while she gyrated rhythmically against him.

With a sexual command she'd never known she possessed, she undid the buttons of his shirt and pulled it open so that she could feast her hungry eyes on his muscle-packed chest with its small, flat brown nipples, perfect targets for stroking thumbs.

He looked at her with blazing desire and rested his big hands on her hips, orchestrating her movements and watching the bounce of her small breasts hungrily.

Lord, if he could he would stretch this moment out like a piece of elastic, but he couldn't. Raw, animal passion was surging through him like a potent drug and as she moved faster on him he felt the first ripples of his climax, then he couldn't contain himself any longer. His massive body responded to her in the only way possible just as she stiffened in her own shuddering orgasm.

Nick pulled her down to him, enjoying the feel of her warm, spent body.

He must have been more damned frustrated than he had ever imagined, because making love had never felt better. Even now, the thought of those breasts squashed against his chest was enough to induce thoughts of making love to her again and again. He kissed the top of her head and closed his eyes. Sleep was beginning to descend on him. Sweet, irresistible sleep. And he could sleep now because he no longer had that wretched anger burning inside of him.

'I can't believe…my God, Nick…how could this have happened?' The full horror of the situation began to dawn on her and reality was like a bucket of freezing water. She pushed herself up and stared down at him, but not for long. She couldn't bring herself to look at his face. And she was glad that he was not looking at her either, his eyes lightly closed. Probably, she thought with another wave of bitter self-recrimination, working out in his head how he could sack her the following Monday without flaunting any obvious company guidelines.

She turned her back on him to dress, her movements jerky, and carried on talking, trying to find some justification for her behaviour.

'I realise this makes our situation very difficult,' she finished, finally getting up the courage to turn around now that she was fully dressed, although under the severe clothing she was all too mortifyingly aware of her body, which was still burning from his caresses. His prone body was swathed in shadow and she was just glad that he was giving her the opportunity to speak. 'I can't begin to tell you how sorry I am…' There was a sob in her voice and she blinked very quickly to clear her head. 'Please don't think I blame you in any way…I don't…I…I blame myself, and I'll understand perfectly if you want me to hand in my resignation on Monday…'

She took a couple of tentative steps closer towards him.

'Nick…?' When he didn't answer she moved towards the sofa and stared down at his relaxed body, one arm slung carelessly over the side of the sofa, the other resting lightly on his chest.

Asleep. Fast asleep.

She remained where she was for a few seconds, wondering whether her need to talk was greater than his need to sleep. After a few more seconds of indecision she sighed softly and put on her coat and scarf, closing the door quietly behind her.

They had both acted on crazy impulse, she thought shakily, except he had an excuse and she had none. It had been an agonising reversal of roles. Wasn't it usually the man who took advantage of the inebriated woman? When he woke up, would he see her as someone who had taken advantage of his temporary defencelessness? It was a sickening, horrifying thought.

If she remained working for him, she at least had learnt her lesson. She would prove to him that her moment of weakness had been a passing madness. She had seen for herself the depth of his raging grief that had allowed him to use her as therapy and she had allowed herself to be used as therapy. She could only now regain her self-respect by ensuring that it never happened again. Ever.

CHAPTER TWO

NICK stood at the floor-to-ceiling window of his office, hands thrust aggressively into his pockets, and stared, scowling, at the grimy London buildings outside.

His entire weekend had been spent reassuring departing relatives that he was fine, that, yes, getting back to work immediately was the right thing for him to do, that, no, he didn't need to get away. On top of that he had had to cope with what had happened on the Friday night.

He muttered an oath to himself and dragged himself away from the unappealing view outside to sit at his desk.

Of course he would have to face Lucy but what he was going to say was another matter. He could scarcely believe what had happened. The recollection had a dream-like quality about it, but, inebriated though he had been, he unfortunately had not been inebriated enough to consign to blissful oblivion the glaring fact that he had lost control. With his secretary. And, worse, the thought nagged away at the back of his mind that somehow she had been forced into doing something she would have found abhorrent.

He gazed abstractedly at his computer terminal and waited.

What, he wondered grimly, had he said to her? Anything? Had he jumped on her? The thought made him slam his fist on his desk in a gesture of frustrated rage that was directed entirely at himself. He almost suspected that she would not turn up at all, and if she failed to do so then he could hardly blame her.

But she did.

Even the prospect of facing him on the Monday morning, terrifying though it was, did not deter her from getting up at the usual time, getting dressed in her usual manner, having what passed for her breakfast, a snatched cup of coffee and a slice of toast.

Lucy only faltered when she was finally standing in front of the glasshouse office building, then she took a deep breath and propelled herself through the revolving door.

She was aware of several of her colleagues greeting her, and she heard herself greeting them in return, wondering feverishly if they could spot anything different about her.

The second floor of the building was designated to the directors of the company. Lucy strode along and when she reached the door to her own office she glanced desperately towards the lift and wondered what it would feel like to just run away.

Maybe he wouldn't be there, she thought to herself, as her nervous apprehension reached stomach-churning levels. Maybe he would have no memory of what had taken place. Temporary amnesia through excessive alcohol. That sort of thing happened quite frequently; she was sure of it.

She pushed open her door, walked in and saw him, sitting in his leather chair, every inch the forbidding, ruthlessly self-assured boss she was accustomed to. He had been staring at his computer but his eyes met hers the minute she walked through the door and Lucy smiled a tentative greeting.

'Would you like a coffee?' she asked, removing her coat and hanging it on the coat stand by the door. When he didn't answer she went to stand by the interconnecting door to his office, hovering indecisively and trying very hard to maintain an air of efficient normality.

'I think we need to have a little chat, don't you?'

So he *had* remembered. Had she really expected otherwise?

'Do we?' Lucy asked in a voice that bordered on the pleading. 'There's so much to do on a Monday morning. Shouldn't I be getting on with work?' Her mouth dried up as his black eyes swept over her.

'Come in and shut the door behind you. I've told Christina to make sure that no calls come through until advised.' He could see the reluctance on her face, could sense her desperate longing for him to say nothing of what had taken place, and another spasm of self-disgust twisted in his gut.

Of all the people in the world, he'd had to get drunk and fall on the one who was least able to handle it. Lucy had never once shown any inclination that she was attracted to him. She was the most private woman he had ever known. Even when he had been married, and very faithfully married despite the provocation, he had been a magnet for other women, including those with husbands tucked safely at their sides. Distasteful though the thought was, he would have preferred to direct his unsteady feet towards the nearest bar and pick up a woman. Anyone other than the girl standing in front of him with her huge, dismayed eyes which she was trying so hard to conceal.

Not only would he have spared her from his despicable behaviour, he would not now be in a position of wondering just how uncontrolled he had been emotionally in front of her.

'Sit down,' he ordered, trying to modulate the tenor of his voice. 'We have to talk about what took place on Friday night.'

'Must we? Wouldn't it be better for us to both forget about it? We're adults. These things happen...' Her voice trailed off into anguished silence, which only made his expression harden as he contemplated the idiotic madness of his behaviour.

'Would you feel more comfortable if we discussed this out of the office?' he asked. 'There's a coffee bar ten minutes' walk away from—'

'No!' Lucy edged towards the chair facing him, the one she used for more mundane reasons such as jotting notes down in her pad. 'This is fine.'

'Right.' Nick sat back in the chair and broodingly surveyed the nervous fair-haired woman in front of him. Where to begin? 'First of all I want to...apologise for what happened between us. My behaviour was inexcusable.' He was visited by a split-second of instant recall, the memory of small breasts spilling from a bra, rosy-peaked nipples against pale, soft skin, and he drew in his breath sharply, dispelling the disturbing image. 'My only excuse is that the situation was...somewhat extraordinary.'

'I realise that,' Lucy said, steeling herself not to wilt. She had seen the expression of disgust cross his face earlier on and it had been all she could do to remain where she was and not run sobbing from the room. He talked about his behaviour and made all the right noises of regret and apology but she could tell that he had found her behaviour as repellent as his own. Her behaviour, she thought with mortification, and her body.

'I had just come from the most traumatic experience of my life…' What the hell had they talked about? He remembered he'd spoken quite honestly with her—just what had he said? They must have talked about *something*. Had he made an even bigger fool of himself by discussing the private details of his married life? Had he, God forbid, broken down? Cried?

No. He rejected the thought completely. He wouldn't have. He simply was not built that way.

'Perhaps I spoke to you about that…?' he prompted in an attempt to fill in the missing pieces.

'No, of course not!' Lucy's denial was spontaneous. 'I… Look, I understand. I understand why you felt that you had to get away. I told you so at the time. You were grief-stricken and you were dealing with it by…by losing yourself in drink.'

So he hadn't confessed anything. Nick breathed an inward sigh of relief.

This was just the tip of the iceberg, however. He had to find out how exactly they had ended up making love.

'Not very appropriate behaviour,' he commented, allowing her to relax, knowing that the minute he broached the whole subject of sex she would revert to her stammering state of utter confusion. He looked down and idly picked up the fountain pen lying on his desk. Despite the advance of technology, he still used a fountain pen for writing letters and signing his name on documents. He twirled it slowly between his fingers now, making sure that he didn't look at her. She seemed to go to pieces whenever he looked at her, something she had never done before. Then again, she had probably never been repelled by him before.

'Have you ever drowned your sorrows, Lucy? Drunk

too much for your own good? Behaved like a complete fool with no regard for the consequences?'

Of course, in retrospect, he would consider himself a fool to have made love with her, she thought with a burning sense of shame and hurt. This conversation would have been totally different if she had been beautiful and sophisticated. In fact, it probably wouldn't have been taking place at all. 'I did get drunk once when I was eighteen but I had such a bad hangover that I never did it again. And, no, I have never had to drown my sorrows in drink. But of course, as I said…'

'What a blameless life you must lead,' Nick mused, half to himself. Of course, it was written on her face, a fresh innocence that he had blasted his way into like a maniac. For the first time he wondered what her outside life was like. It had never occurred to him before, but then he had been so wrapped up in his own personal domestic nightmare that he had spent very little time actually noticing the people around them. He moved through them, did deals, went to meetings and functioned in a way that had been utterly detached from any curiosity.

Oddly, he found himself sidetracked by questions that had nothing to do with why he had called her into his office.

'What do you do out of work?' he asked suddenly and Lucy looked at him in surprise.

'What do I do out of work? What do you mean?'

'Do you go out much? Do you share a house with other people? Is that why you decided to come to the office on Friday? Because you couldn't face your housemates?' She hadn't been a virgin, he thought suddenly. He had another vivid image of her lying on him, her breasts swinging above his face as she moved, her slight body grinding against his hard, pulsing masculinity. His body stirred in response and he clenched his jaw at the intrusive thoughts.

'No, no, I don't share a house. In fact, I have my own flat. In a renovated Victorian house that's been converted into ten flats. It's not in the best part of London, but it does.'

'And do you go out much?'

'I have a normal social life,' Lucy informed him, tilting her chin up defensively. It would have been a hell of a lot more normal if she hadn't spent precious time hankering after the man facing her. She cringed at the thought that he might ever find out that little fact. She, at least, had not once uttered a word about how disastrously attracted she had always been by him. She had not allowed her short-sighted passion to guide her words. And he would never find out.

'I go to the movies with friends, go to the theatre now and again, have meals out…'

'With men?' he asked smoothly, picking up on her list of hobbies and tacking on what purported to be a natural follow-on question.

'Sometimes.'

'And do you have a lover?' It was an outrageously interfering question, he thought to himself, but curiosity had got the better of him. Sex with her had been good. Better than good. Or so it seemed to him in hazy retrospect. But her demure appearance belied any such suggestion.

Yes, you, once in reality but a thousand times in my head. 'I don't think that's any of your business,' Lucy said, half-shocked by the directness of her statement.

'You are quite right,' Nick said soothingly. 'I am perfectly sure that if you had you would never have…' The silence, fraught with the unspoken, stretched between them.

'No,' Lucy blurted out.

'Which brings me to something that I have been turning over and over in my mind all weekend.'

She knew exactly what he was going to say. He was going to ask her why she had ever allowed herself to have sex with him and she frantically sought in her head for the answer that would be furthest away from the humiliating truth, which was that she had simply been unable to resist, that all her pent-up yearning had broken down her usual powers of reason and common sense and left her mindlessly drifting in a sea of sensuality. He had touched her and she had been lost, totally and shamelessly lost.

'What's that?' she asked faintly.

'Why?'

For a few desperate seconds, Lucy pretended to be bewildered by his question.

'Why…what?' she asked finally, buying time.

'Why did you? You were working peacefully here, albeit at an extraordinarily peculiar time, and I lurched in… I confess I am surprised that you did not flee the building in terror.'

'I…I'm not the fleeing-buildings type of girl,' she answered in a high-pitched voice. 'Besides, I knew who you were and I could see that you had been drinking. I only thought to make sure that you didn't pass out, to be honest.' All the truth so far.

'And…?' He couldn't find the words to phrase the question but it was vitally important that he knew the truth, that he had not coerced her into a situation against her will. He could not seriously believe that he was capable of any such thing, but the demon drink could work in a thousand ways, and he was not accustomed to consuming large amounts of it.

'Look,' he said impatiently, 'I need to find out whether I...took advantage of you in any way...'

'Took advantage?'

'And stop repeating every phrase I utter. You know precisely what I mean. Did I force you to do something against your will?' His body went still as he waited for her to reply. If his memory served him right...but he couldn't rely on his memory.

'No,' Lucy told him quietly.

'Then did I somehow use my position to influence you in any way?' His razor-sharp memory was failing him just when he needed it most. 'Did I hint that you might...I don't know...lose your job if...?'

'No. Don't you think I have a mind of my own?' she flared, insulted by the insinuation that she would either do something against her will or else yield to something simply for the sake of a job.

'Of course I do,' Nick grated harshly. 'I am merely trying to establish what precisely happened.'

'What for?' Lucy blurted out, her face reddening. She could feel tears pricking the backs of her eyelids and swallowed them down. 'What's the point in performing a post-mortem on what happened? I was perfectly prepared to...to pretend...'

'That nothing had happened? Be an ostrich that sticks its head in the sand? I needed to talk to you about this because you happen to be my secretary and if either of us felt that we no longer had a tenable working situation then I would be obliged to transfer you to another position within the company.'

Just like that, Lucy thought bitterly. If he thought that he had done something dishonourable, then he would have given her the push. Their act of making love, the memory of which could still turn her bones to water, whatever she felt about herself for doing what she had done, was less than nothing to him. He might call her an ostrich, but she wasn't. Far from it. She could feel the impact of reality crashing into her like an avalanche.

'I'm perfectly happy to resign if you don't think you can work with me,' she said coolly.

'That is not what I'm saying…'

'No? It sounds that way to me.'

'And you can say, with your hand on your heart, that you can behave as though none of this had ever happened?'

'Yes.' She managed to find sufficient resources of control to utter the lie with a perfectly bland expression. 'As you said, it happened and, yes, it never should have, but it did.'

'Perhaps because you wanted it to?' Nick asked slyly, and his suggestion was so close to the truth that for a split-second she could feel her body freeze, then a sudden, flaring heat thawed it out and galvanised her into action.

'If you really want to know,' she said coldly, 'I did it because I felt sorry for you.'

Nick had thrown out his taunt like an arrow in the dark, never thinking that he might hit the target. Obscurely, the idea that she might have wanted him, have actively wanted to sleep with him, had had the astounding effect of turning him on. Her reply now stopped him in his tracks.

She had felt sorry for him. Of course. It made perfect sense. He had shown up unexpectedly, in a pathetic state, and she had been overwhelmed by pity. The thought cut through every ounce of pride he had and his expression hardened.

'I was overcome and I acted stupidly. I just got carried away with…with pity—pity and compassion for the pain I knew you must be feeling.'

'No one has ever pitied me in my life before,' Nick said harshly. He linked his fingers together and pressed his thumbs into the palms of his hands. *Pity.* The word conjured up images of vulnerability and weakness that he found revolting. At least when applied to him.

'Perhaps because you've never been in a position to incite such an emotion,' Lucy told him, warming to her subject now that she had found herself unexpectedly saved from having the truth forced out of her. 'You were in a black hole and…'

'And, out of the goodness of your heart, you thought you might shine a little ray of light.'

'No,' she denied, 'not out of the goodness of my heart. It just seemed natural at the time. But I can see that it was wrong, all wrong, and for that I apologise.'

He wondered savagely whether she had enjoyed dispensing her cure or whether she had simply been swept away by the emotion of the moment.

Well, he could hardly ask her to resign now. That would have been tantamount to declaring that he was too weak to deal with what had taken place.

'Yes, it was wrong,' he said, forcing some semblance of calm assurance into his voice, 'and I want you to know that under normal circumstances there is no way in the world that I would ever dream of sleeping with you.' It was an aggressively phrased remark, taut with implications, and he knew that he was hitting below the belt. In truth, he had had no idea that this meeting would progress along these lines. He'd thought that he would subtly find out what he needed to know, namely that he had not forced himself upon her, and then he would close the book and lay that particular chapter to rest.

He had not reckoned on being drawn into this type of discussion. He had pressed for the truth, though, not satisfied with the obviously genuine reassurances she had given him, and he had discovered that the truth was not to his liking.

Now, obscurely, he was not prepared to lay the matter to rest. He stood up and began prowling restlessly around the room, looking at her from various angles while she kept her head perfectly still and staring straight towards the window behind his desk.

'Of course,' he said lazily, pausing to inspect the rows of books that he kept on the shelves on one side of the office; he ran his fingers delicately along the hardbound spines, then turned to face her, 'I hope you do not misinterpret this in any way. I merely want you to know that there will be no repetition of what took place, of that you may be sure.'

Lucy wondered how many more ways there could be for him to dress up the obvious behind lots of protective packaging. He was telling her that he did not find her attractive. She had been a warm body at a time when he had needed it and, fool that she was, she had succumbed because her heart had won the battle with her head. But that was it. In a sober state, she was as sexless as the two framed prints he had hanging on his wall.

'Oh, good,' she said flatly, her face still averted so that he was unable to see the expression in her eyes. And her eyes were very expressive. He was surprised that he had not noticed that before. Huge brown eyes framed with long, dark brown eyelashes that somehow seemed at odds with the blondeness of her hair and the paleness of her skin.

He shook his head irritably and walked back to his chair, but instead of sitting down he stood behind it, leaning casually against the high back, his forearms hanging loosely over the front.

Oh, good? Was that all she had to say on the subject?

'You're not my type,' he informed her, lowering his eyes and missing the hurt wince that had Lucy drawing her breath in on a hiss.

He might think that spelling it out would somehow make her more comfortable, put her mind at rest that she had nothing to fear from him should they find themselves working late together in an empty building, as they often had in the past.

He was wrong. Every word he uttered was another nail in her heart.

She looked at him, at his dauntingly beautiful face. She knew every groove of that face as though it were her own. Had committed it to memory, even though she had tried hard not to.

No, she wouldn't be his type. She was as physically ordinary as he was impressively, compellingly handsome. He would always be drawn to women like his wife. Stunningly beautiful women with big hair and breasts.

She fancied she saw something ruefully patronising in his expression.

'And I feel I ought to make this clear if we are to resume our working relationship,' he continued slowly, frowning, as if uncertain as to how he should say what he had to say.

What more? she wondered numbly.

For a few seconds, Nick didn't go on. He simply

looked at her assessingly, as if weighing up in his mind whether he should proceed or not, then he sighed.

'Perhaps this is something best left unsaid.'

Lucy drew her lips together in a stubborn line. 'If you feel you have something further to add then I really do wish that you would tell me. I've been very…happy working here and, as you say, we have to clear the air if we can continue our working relationship…' She could be as coolly controlled as he could, she thought to herself. The fact was that she loved what she did, whether Nick was her boss or not. She enjoyed the work and she doubted she would ever have been able to find a job that paid as well anywhere else in London.

'All right.' He shrugged his broad shoulders with typically Mediterranean expressiveness and swung his chair around, turning it to face her once he was sitting. 'If you insist…'

'I insist.'

'You are young and I would not want you to harbour any notions that our few hours together might be the start of an agenda. Nor would I wish you to think that you are now somehow privileged in any way whatsoever. You are an excellent secretary and I personally feel that it is imperative that we maintain the boundaries between us.'

'In other words, you're cautioning me not to rip my clothes off and fling myself at you,' Lucy said slowly, appalled at his line of thinking.

The disparaging tone of her voice, which only just managed to escape being insolent, was not sufficient for his mind to ignore the image she had presented of herself. Wild, abandoned, coming towards him with her arms outstretched and her naked, creamy body offering itself for his inspection. For his lingering exploration.

The image sent a rush of heat to his loins and he compensated for that by frowning coldly at her.

'Not precisely my words...'

'As good as,' Lucy clarified brutally. 'You can rest assured that I won't, *sir*.'

'There is no need to labour the point.' Nick flushed darkly, fully aware of how he had sounded.

'Nor,' she continued, steamrolling over his interruption and barely managing to keep her voice steady, 'will I suddenly think that I can swan in and out and do as I please because we made a mistake. I won't.' Never before had she deviated from her role of efficient secretary, willing to put in whatever hours were asked of her without complaint. Nor had she ever verbally struck out at him, as she was doing now, and it felt good. Good to be letting some of her crushing hurt spill out in anger. If she had to, she could get another job. It might pay half the amount she earned working for him, but at least she would be free of his presence and the havoc he wreaked on her heart without even being aware of it.

'And just for the record,' she flung at him, making no attempt to lower her voice, 'you are no more my type than I am yours!'

'So, you make a habit of sleeping with men you don't like?' He should have closed the conversation. Instead he found himself prolonging it, his dark face flushed and scowling.

'No,' Lucy sighed, 'that's not what I said at all. And I apologise for...well, for speaking my mind out of turn.' She ran her fingers through her short blonde hair and then linked them together on her lap. 'The circumstances were, as you said, extraordinary. I like you well enough, and I respect you, but you're not the sort of man I would normally...normally...'

'Be attracted to?' Nick enquired silkily.

'If you want to put it that way.' Thank goodness she wasn't Pinocchio, she thought, or her nose would be reaching the other side of the office by now.

'And what sort of man *are* you attracted to?'

'Look,' Lucy said, horrified that she had overstepped the mark with no thought for what he had so recently gone through. As if, at this point in time, he really cared one way or another about her or what she thought! Just another instance of how easy it was for her to lose touch with reality when he was around. 'Look, I'm sorry. This is the wrong time for us to be pursuing this conversation. You must have had a hellish weekend and you certainly do not need to come in here to work to have a hellish morning.' She attempted a soothing, understanding smile.

'You still haven't answered my question.'

'No, I haven't,' she said in the same soothing voice, which appeared to be having no effect whatsoever. 'But, if you really want to know, I'm attracted to...nice, thoughtful, caring men...'

'Nice. Thoughtful. Caring.'

'Not,' she amended hastily, 'that you aren't. I'm sure you're all of those things.'

'But you wouldn't want to stake your house on it,' Nick said drily, forcing a reluctant smile from her.

'Maybe not,' Lucy agreed.

This was as close to a truce as they could get, she realised. Now the air had been cleared and work could begin. He had said his piece, she had said hers and she knew instinctively that every word spoken between them would remain behind these four walls.

'So...' Nick sat back and extracted a file in front of him '...I want you to get some letters out for this lot.

I've already dictated three into the machine. You'll need to transcribe those, and, with this one, just write and question some of the bills we've been charged. Find out whether our guy in Boston checked out all the suppliers before he placed this particular order. It just seems a little excessive to me...'

He watched as she stood up and bent over to take the file from him.

Everything back to normal. Except...he couldn't help his eyes from drifting towards the neckline of her blouse, following it down to where, as she straightened, it fell softly over her breasts. Everything about her appearance was neat and smart, but there was a fire burning there. He had sensed it during their conversation and he could almost catch hold of wisps of memory about the Friday before, teasing little recollections of her moaning hotly as he had touched her.

Nick shook his head.

Not each other's type. That much was true. His type, from as far back as when he had been an adolescent, was along Gina's lines. Voluptuously built women with long hair and bodies that swayed with blatant sexuality.

And Lucy... His eyes drifted back towards her. Yes, he could see that she would be attracted to the clean-cut, boy-next-door kind of man, someone pleasant, easy-going, nice. Dull, in other words.

He turned his chair at an angle so that he had his profile towards her and stared absent-mindedly through the large window.

'Are you all right?'

Nick inclined his head towards Lucy, who had gathered her various files and was standing hesitantly by the chair in which she had previously been sitting.

'What did you think of Gina?' he asked curiously.

'You met her a few times over the months you've been working with me. What did you think of her?'

The question threw Lucy, not least because she had never felt a great deal of empathy towards the woman. She had always assumed that that was because she was, quite simply, Nick's wife.

'She was amazingly beautiful,' Lucy told him truthfully.

'Disregard her looks for a moment.'

'Well...I can't say I ever really had any long conversations with her.'

'You didn't like her, did you?'

'Yes, of course I did!' She flushed hotly and he cast a jaundiced, sidelong look at her for a few brief seconds.

Of course she hadn't liked her, he thought with blinding clarity. Gina had never been the sort of woman who had felt the need to cultivate the friendship of other women. They would never have been able to give her the undiluted attention she craved. He couldn't remember her having any close female friends, simply wives of wealthy men whose company she maintained because they had been a necessary part of her vital social life.

'Did you?' he murmured more to himself than to her, and Lucy held herself very still, straining forward to catch his words. 'My mother never approved, you know.' Another confidence that he now somehow found himself compelled to confess. 'She thought that Gina and I weren't suited. As far as she was concerned, Gina was too flamboyant.'

'Which just goes to show that love can survive other people's opinions,' Lucy said stoically. 'Parents can be very critical when it comes to their children's partners,' she continued lamely when he failed to reply.

Nick sighed and swivelled round to face her. 'Now, I

would bet that you have never given your parents any cause to be critical.'

Lucy looked at his dark, handsome face, each hard line and angle a revelation of power and beauty, his every movement as economically graceful as an athlete's, and she thought that her parents would be vastly critical were they ever to find out what had taken place between their well-behaved, respectable daughter and her charismatic boss. Shocked and critical.

'No,' she said, turning away. 'Is that all? Shall I get back to work now?'

'Yes. I think we have said all there is to say.'

'I think we have,' Lucy agreed quietly. 'And I would be grateful if…if no more is mentioned about…'

'Our little mistake. I quite agree.' Nick tapped the keyboard of his computer and it whirred softly into gear. He barely glanced as she left his office, gently closing the door behind her.

CHAPTER THREE

THE trip in to work this morning had been worse than usual. Lucy had missed her usual tube, had had to wait twenty minutes before she could get on the next one, and when she had managed to squeeze into a compartment had had to spend the entire thirty-minute journey hanging onto the pole by the door so that she was constantly buffeted by people getting in and getting off at every stop.

And on top of that she had the first stirrings of a sore throat, which probably meant that she was coming down with a cold.

So she was not in the best of moods when she finally made it to her office to find Nick waiting for her.

'You're late.'

Lucy calmly hung her lightweight jacket on the coat stand by the door and turned around to look at him. The connecting door between their offices was flung open and he was sitting behind his desk with his chair pushed well back so that he could stretch out his long legs at an angle. He looked as though he had been there for hours already, even though it was only a little after nine. His white shirt was rolled to the elbows and his tie had been loosened so that he could undo the first two buttons of his shirt.

'I'm sorry. I slept through my alarm clock and then I missed my tube and had to wait ages before I could get on another one. Shall I sort out the post and bring it in to you?'

'Just get in here. With your notepad.' He watched her through the open door as she walked towards her desk, leant over and fished out her pad from the drawer on the right-hand side.

Sometimes the line of her jaw when she turned her head or the flick of her wrist took him spinning back over eight months to when they had made love, right here on the sofa in his own office. When that happened he was left feeling oddly shaken and disoriented. It was as if his mind was holding out something for him to take, but, whatever that something was, it was just a little too far out of reach.

He abruptly dragged his eyes away from her slender body, now straightening with notepad obediently in one hand and pen in the other.

'Can I expect you in here before the year is out?' he rasped, pulling himself towards the desk and flicking through some files in front of him.

'Sorry.' Lucy hurried in, flustered, and took her seat opposite him, poised to take notes.

'If you don't think you can function properly today, then it's better if you have the day off and send Terri in to cover for you.'

'I'm fine.'

'Have there been any developments with this Rawlings business?' he asked, glancing up at her.

Even now that her life was seemingly swimming along, she still couldn't look at him without that stirring of awareness, as forbidden now as it had been when he had been married and out of bounds.

'We received a fax from them yesterday evening. Actually I stuck it on your desk.'

'Just tell me what it said,' Nick told her shortly, frowning.

'Another dip in profits. No reason given. The usual optimistic forecasts for the next six months and no excuse as to why the past six months have been so sluggish.'

'And you phoned Rawlings himself?'

'He was out.'

'Out where?'

'I don't know,' Lucy said with a rebellious tide of irritation at his attitude. What was the matter with him? Even for him, this was more of a foul mood than normal. 'Perhaps we could employ someone to act as an undercover agent and track his every movement.'

Nick regarded her narrowly, noting the slow flush spreading along her cheekbones. Hell, he knew he was being aggressive, unnecessarily so, but he couldn't stop himself. It had been like this for the past eight months. She had seen a side to him that had never been revealed to the public eye, had seen him at his most vulnerable, and some demon in him now drove him to punish her for that.

Lord, he knew that he should just have her transferred to another department. There were enough of them to choose from. He could raise her pay extravagantly to make the move justified and irresistible, but whenever he thought of walking into the office and not being able to see her he weakened and told himself that he needed to hang on to her, that she was the best secretary he could ever hope for.

'I don't believe I pay you to be sarcastic,' he informed her coolly and, without waiting for an answer, proceeded to give his undivided attention to the Rawlings fax in front of him. 'This doesn't make any sense,' he continued, while she simmered away in the chair, hating him and hating herself even more for the fact that he could get to her every time. 'The hotel should be harvesting money. It is on an island, in the sun, good airline connections from the US, no political instability. So what the hell is going on? Dammit, I should have handled this one myself instead of handing it over to Bob. What does he have to say about this? No, better still, I'll get him on the line. Stay here so that I can dictate a letter to you when I'm through with Bob.'

Lucy let her eyes wander as she listened to Nick speak curtly down the phone to his financial director. She was aware of him leaning forward as he spoke, his brows meeting in a slight frown, his black hair shorter than it was when she had run her fingers through it, and combed neatly back. His restless energy manifested itself in the tapping of his fountain pen on the sheaf of paper in front of him. After a few minutes he dropped the receiver back in its handset and sat back in the leather swivel chair to look at her.

'Take this letter,' he ordered. His dictation was always faultless. He composed fluently and without any need for her to make revisions. He was one of the few people whose clarity of thought was translated into clarity of speech without any hesitancy or confusion along the way.

When she stood up to leave he snapped impatiently, 'Sit back down. I haven't finished with you as yet.' God, but he could shake her out of that docility! His eyes involuntarily moved to her breasts, totally hidden behind her neat shirt with its severe little row of buttons and prim rounded collar, and he looked away immediately. Unwelcome thoughts had a nasty habit of creeping up on him when he was least expecting it, thoughts of ripping off her shirt and scooping those breasts out of their constraints so that he could taste them once again, prove once and for all whether their lovemaking had been as magnificent as his hazy memory recalled, or whether that had been an illusion.

'I want you to order some flowers to be sent for me.'

'Flowers?' Lucy's hand froze momentarily over her notepad, then she plastered her usual bland smile on her face.

'You heard me. Flowers.'

'Right. What kind of flowers?'

Nick shrugged nonchalantly. 'You tell me...what kind of flowers does a woman like? Roses? Violets? Orchids? Anything, but make it expensive.'

'And should there be a message to accompany the flowers?' She knew that there had been women in the past few months. He had made no effort to conceal his love life from her, and from what she had deduced his love life was very hectic indeed. But never before had she been requested to act as a link between him and any of his women and the thought of that made her feel ill.

'Just "*Thanks for the good times.*"' He had pushed his chair back so that his profile was to her and he was staring out of the window.

'"*Thanks for the good times,*"' Lucy repeated. 'Nothing else?'

'What else is there to say when a relationship comes to an end?' Nick asked with an edge of sarcasm.

'Nothing.' She snapped shut her notepad. 'Will that be all?'

'Are you in some kind of hurry to go? Urgent ten o'clock appointment somewhere?'

'Just a lot of work to get through before I leave this afternoon,' Lucy answered vaguely.

'Which reminds me. I have scheduled a meeting with Bob this evening at six to discuss what the hell is going on with the Tradewinds Hotel and Rawlings. I will want you to stay so that you can take notes.'

'I'm sorry. I can't.'

Nick swivelled his chair so that he was now facing her. *'Can't?'* He pronounced the single word as though it belonged to some little-used foreign dialect and Lucy flushed and looked away. This was a first for her.

'I've made plans for this evening…'

'In which case you can cancel them. Bob is flying to the Far East tomorrow and I want this Rawlings business sorted out before he goes and I need you here.'

'I'm sorry,' she apologised again, 'perhaps I can arrange for Terri to work late and I can transcribe the notes tomorrow morning when I come in.'

'What are you doing that is so important?' he demanded. He stood up and began prowling through the office, hands thrust into his trouser pockets. Out of the corner of his eye he could see her trying hard to formulate a suitable reply, staring straight ahead as if afraid that one unwary move might bring her eyes clashing to his. Good ploy, he thought with a sudden, savage sourness, but not good enough.

He came to stand directly in front of her, so that she had nowhere to turn without seeing him, and to further ram home his presence he leant forward, propping his hands on either side of her chair and effectively forming an unassailable cage.

'Well?' he enquired. 'Part of the unwritten agreement between myself and my secretary is the understanding that overtime is a given. As and when. It is why you are paid so exorbitantly.'

'And I've never let you down before!' Lucy raised her eyes to his and flinched back at the proximity. She couldn't focus her thoughts properly when he was this close. In fact, her head felt as though it was stuffed with cotton wool.

He continued to stare at her in thunderous silence, watching her wriggle like a worm on a hook and ferociously determined to find out just what the hell was so important that she couldn't stay for an extra two hours after work.

'I'm going out with…someone,' Lucy finally admitted. 'We made an arrangement to go to the theatre and it's been hard work getting hold of these tickets, and afterwards we're going out for a meal.'

'You are going out with someone,' Nick said flatly. He pushed himself away, only to perch on the edge of his desk so that she had an uninterrupted view of his thighs and his linked fingers resting lightly on them. 'In other words, you are going on a date.'

Lucy felt a surge of anger and she lowered her eyes to hide the fiery glint in them.

She was going on a date and he made it sound as though she were making arrangements for a bank robbery. Had he imagined all these months that she had been hankering after him? Did he think that he could sleep with however many countless women he wanted but that she was too dull to expect more than a one-night stand with a man who had had too much to drink and was wrapped up in the throes of mourning?

Robert might not be the most scintillating of companions but they had a laugh together and their relationship had a certain gentle quality that was soothing to her raw nerves.

'Yes, I'm going on a date.'

'And how long has this been going on?'

'How long has *what* been going on?' Lucy asked incredulously.

'How long have you been seeing this man? It *is* just the one man, I take it? Or are there more lurking in the background?' Nick knew how he sounded. Like an arrogant bore poking his nose into something that was no business of his. In fact, he should be delighted that she was dating. If nothing else it would kill for once and for all that niggling suspicion that she had somehow managed to crawl under his skin and was lodged there waiting for him to make the next move. He had spent the past few months in total control of the situation, never referring to their little mistake. He was back to controlling his love life, picking up and discarding women with admirable ease. With a lover in the background, his secretary would be out of bounds and his mind, which had a habit of straying at inappropriate times, would be harnessed.

Unfortunately, he felt not in the slightest bit relieved.

'There's just the one man,' she snapped back, unable to resist. 'I don't make it a habit to play the field.'

'Is that a comment on my lifestyle?'

Lucy focused intently on the redundant notepad on her lap. Her skin was crawling with a painful, heightened sensitivity to the man glaring down at her. How could Robert ever hope to compete with what this man did to her? she wondered with anguish. The prepared answer sprang to mind: Robert might not be the charged powerhouse that Nick Constantinou was, but his very muted affability was far more suited to her. The thought gave her the courage to meet his eyes squarely.

'No, it's not.' Yes, it was, but she'd be damned if she would become embroiled in a discussion about his love life. It had caused her enough sleepless nights as it was, knowing that he was seeing someone, connecting calls from women, reading about him in the gossip columns in which he appeared to have gained the dubious status of London's most desirable bachelor. He was trying to forget his wife in the arms of a succession of women, all of whom, from what she had glimpsed, were of the statuesque-model category. Good for him.

Nick could quite happily have wrung her neck. Instead he fulminated in silence for a few minutes before reining in his straying mind.

'So, what is this lucky man's name?'

'Robert.'

'And how did you meet him? Don't surprise me further by telling me that you met him in a nightclub.'

'Because nightclubs are a little risqué for me?' Lucy enquired tartly. 'I met him at a dinner party. He was introduced to me and we hit it off.'

'You hit it off.' He casually strolled back to his chair and sat down. 'And what does this Robert fellow do?'

'Do?'

'For a living,' Nick embellished with a little spurt of intense irritation. 'I take it he has a job and doesn't spend his days sitting on a park bench feeding the ducks?'

'He's a financial controller at a large company.'

'Ah. An accountant.'

Lucy gritted her teeth and decided not to pursue the argumentative carrot being dangled in front of her. Every word he was saying was making her hackles rise a little bit more and she was determined not to explode.

'At any rate, that's the reason I can't stay behind to work this evening. I'll get Terri sorted out. What time do you want her to be here?'

'Quarter to six. Enough time for me to fill her in a bit about this little problem.' He paused and rested his elbows thoughtfully on the desk. 'What play are you going to see?' he asked conversationally, his attention already appearing to stray as he flicked through a file in front of him.

'Oh, that musical at the Apollo. It's very popular at the moment.' She stood up and added with a spurt of malice. 'Robert has one or two connections in the theatre world, hence the tickets.'

'Oh, how nice. And where are you going to eat afterwards? Anywhere exciting?'

Exciting? Me? Lucy wanted to exclaim, *Good heavens, no. My heart might collapse under the strain of anything exciting.* 'There's a French restaurant in Covent Garden. Café Benedict. We're going there. I'll tell Terri about this evening.' She hovered, waiting for some last command, but he seemed to have forgotten her presence in the office and she quickly exited, back to the relative sanctuary of her own four walls and computer terminal.

He was still submerged in work when she left the office at five, barely looking up to glance at her, and Lucy scuttled off before he could tear himself away from his computer long enough to decide that he preferred her note-taking abilities to Terri's. Over the past eight months she had assumed more responsibility with their clients than she had before, and as a source of information she was far superior to the other secretary, whose duties were more heavily tied in with the accounting side of the business.

As a reaction to the effect Nick had had on her earlier on in the day, Lucy made a special effort with her dress for Robert. It was balmy outside, so there was no need for a jacket, and instead she wore a clinging long-sleeved jersey dress in a rich coffee colour that fell just to mid-thigh, and a pair of high, backless sandals. Hell to walk in for any distance but charmingly appropriate to the occasion.

And Robert was gratifyingly pleased with the result. He greeted her at the door with a bunch of white carnations and gave her a long, low wolf-whistle that made Lucy burst out laughing.

'Wrong response,' Robert said, following her into her living room and waiting while she stuck the flowers into a vase of water, fiddling with the stems until she had manoeuvred them into a satisfactory display. 'You should have swooned.'

'I will in a minute,' Lucy teased back, 'just as soon as I've finished with these flowers.'

This was more like it, she told herself firmly as she sat in the darkened theatre, her fingers loosely entwined with his. She had been seeing Robert for only three months, but she knew that he was a gentleman. He had not forced himself upon her once, allowing her to take the lead. They conversed easily, with no uncomfortable lapses in the conversation, and although they had only kissed she was sure that when the time came and it was right to make love to him it would be as gentle and fulfilling as she hoped. Nothing like the searing roller-coaster ride she had had with Nick.

Just the memory of that was enough to make her shiver, and Robert squeezed his fingers affectionately around hers, leaning across to murmur something about the play.

'We should do this more often,' Robert said to her later as he hailed a black cab to take them to the restaurant they had booked. 'Somehow the theatre is exciting in a way the cinema never could be.'

Lucy looked at him and smiled. He really was very good-looking, she thought. Quite a catch. Her parents would definitely approve. They had always approved of anyone who shared the same genes of respectability that they had. She wickedly wondered what they would make of Nick and decided that they would probably reel out the garlic, cross themselves and call for a priest to send him away.

'It's just so bloody difficult getting away from work,' Robert was saying, holding the cab door open so that she could slide past him into the back seat.

'Tell me about it. I had to put my foot down about working late tonight. My boss had decided that he needed me to stay behind and sit in on a meeting with one of the directors of the company.'

Robert nodded sympathetically. 'He should always give you notice if he needs you to work late. That's what I do with my secretary. After all, they've got lives too.'

'I guess,' Lucy said, feeling oddly defensive, 'it's a bit different with Nick. I think it's the way he's built. He thinks nothing of working until three in the morning if the need arises, and so he just assumes that his staff share his feelings about overtime.' In fact, she had twice arrived at work at eight-thirty to find him unshaven and drinking black coffee, having stayed at the office all night. More impressively, he had still been able to function for the remainder of the day.

'Workaholic.' Robert nodded as though it was a concept with which he was fully familiar. 'You get some of those in my profession,' he confided, dipping his fair head towards hers in a gesture of shared understanding, 'work all the hours God made and forget what it's like to enjoy themselves.'

Lucy thought with a smirk that if there was one man on the face of the earth who knew what it was like to enjoy himself, then it was Nick Constantinou. After what seemed to her an indecently short period of mourning, he had thrown himself into London's élite social circles with grim determination.

'Me,' Robert said in a satisfied voice, 'I prefer to afford my working life just as much as I absolutely need to without, of course, jeopardising my promotional chances, and then spend the rest of my time relaxing. Like tonight.'

Lucy could feel his bright eyes on her but her mind was too busy buzzing with images of her boss and his ability to burn the candle at both ends.

'Theatre,' he mused, gently pulling her to him and putting his arm around her shoulders, 'supper and a beautiful companion. Does it get better?'

'Hardly beautiful, but thank you very much.' She smiled and tilted her face up to his, closing her eyes as his mouth softly touched hers.

'Beautiful. It's what I told my mother, who's dying to meet you. I think she can already hear wedding bells ringing.'

Lucy sat up and looked at him quizzically. 'Wedding bells? We've only known each other for a few months!'

'Which is what I told her, but you know mothers. I'm thirty-one and she's already beginning to think that if I don't get a move-on she might not live to see the grandchildren she wants.'

Lucy laughed unsteadily. 'I thought only women worried about their biological clocks!'

'Oh, quite so, although I would prefer to be a father in my thirties than in my sixties.' His voice was lightly teasing but there was a gravity in his expression when he looked at her that made her suspect that his mother's wishes might not be too far removed from his own. 'What's the point fathering a child if you're too old to lift him up?'

Lucy laughed and turned away. 'Point taken. Anyway, tell me about this restaurant we're going to. Have you been there before? I hope it's not one of those pretentious little French places where you have to spend hours trying to decipher the menu. My French is hopeless.'

'No need to worry. I'm fluent in French. I can translate for you. Now admit it: I'm a pretty good catch.'

'I admit it, you're a pretty good catch.' With a certain amount of relief she realised that the taxi was slowing in front of the restaurant and there was no further opportunity to continue their conversation.

'It's a club?' Lucy turned to him questioningly as soon as they were inside. Tables were ranged in semi-darkness around an intimate dance floor and, on a raised podium behind, a jazz band was softly playing a familiar number. 'You didn't tell me you were taking me to a club! I would have dressed a little more...'

'Sexily?' Robert grinned and held her against him for a moment so that he could breathe into her hair. 'You don't know how sexy you look in that dress, Luce. It's very conventional, very elegant, but also very figure-hugging—and believe me that's a very sexy combination. Besides, it's not quite a club. More a restaurant with a little something extra.'

'So we can trip the light fantastic after we've eaten? Burn off some calories?'

'If I didn't have two left feet.'

His unassuming modesty made her laugh and on impulse she curved her arms around his waist and rested her head lightly on his shoulder as they were shown to their table. She felt relaxed and contented, and even more so after a couple of glasses of wine and the very good halibut steak she had ordered. The band had jazzed up its tempo, Robert was saying all the right flattering things in between chatting about the various plays he had seen over the past year, and she was feeling rather sexy when he nuzzled against her neck and slipped his arm over her flat stomach, caressing it through the fine, flimsy material.

'So,' he murmured, 'you never answered my question...'

'Question? What question?'

'The one about us making this a permanent thing.'

'Permanent?' Lucy squeaked and then cleared her throat. 'Robert, we've only known each other for a few months!'

'Which is long enough for me to know that I've found the woman I want to spend the rest of my life with.'

She edged away from him.

'You did say that I was a good catch,' he pointed out, smiling.

'You *are* a good catch.'

'Is that a yes?'

'It's a...a...' Her words petered out in a welter of confusion and she looked at him objectively from under her lashes. Fair hair, blue eyes, a body that benefited from his frequent games of squash, a smiling face that promised just the sort of thoughtful kindness she had imagined would be the ideal antidote to the senseless cravings of her heart. He would make an ideal husband. He would always be dependable, would help out with the children, cook meals when she was tired. He was restful.

'It's a...?' he prompted, interrupting her private contemplations.

'It's an I shall have to think about it,' Lucy answered truthfully. 'You know me, Robert, you know how sensible I am. I just don't think I can give you an answer on the spot...'

'An answer to what?' The familiar, darkly velvety voice was such an unexpected intrusion that for a few seconds Lucy thought that she had imagined it, then Nick circled their table so that he was within their line of vision.

'What are *you* doing here?' Lucy gasped. She had to speak loudly to make herself heard above the music and she looked around quickly to see whether she could spot his party but he appeared to be on his own.

He had changed out of his work clothes and was in a pair of cream trousers with a pale-coloured shirt that emphasised his dark colouring, and she could feel her heart begin to pound.

This was just the sort of reaction that had made her so determined to find someone, someone she could love and who could love her in return. She didn't *need* to deal with this wild, irrational attraction on a daily basis. It wasn't doing her any good.

'Oh, I ended up staying at the office longer than I anticipated, and then I thought that I'd try the food here. I remembered you had mentioned this place and, actually, I thought that you might have left already.'

'Robert.' Lucy turned to the bemused man sitting next to her. 'I seem to have forgotten my manners. This is Nick Constantinou, my boss.'

Comprehension dawned in Robert's blue eyes and he smiled happily, extending his hand. 'So you're the big, bad wolf who keeps my girl working all the hours God made.' He had half risen from his chair to shake the other man's hand, and with a little start Lucy realised that the two men must roughly be the same age, although it was hard to imagine. Robert looked like a fresh-faced young boy next to Nick.

'Is that what she tells you?' Nick looked at her with a lazy smile.

'Are you here with anyone?' Lucy asked politely by way of response and he shrugged vaguely in the direction of the opposite side of the room, which was so crowded that it was impossible for her to follow the direction of his gaze.

'You are not dancing,' he pointed out.

'Blame me.' Robert laughed and looked affectionately at Lucy. 'Luce wanted to dance but I told her that I was born with two left feet. If we went on the dance floor, I think Management would be forced to chuck us out for being a health hazard to the other dancers.' He laughed and Lucy smiled nervously back at him. Her feeling of relaxation had disappeared. First had been Robert's astounding marriage proposal and now this, Nick Constantinou showing up here, obviously with the intention of seeing the man who had had the temerity to have a date with her on a night when she had been asked to work overtime. Maybe he thought that she had been lying about her movements and he had decided to check it out himself, like a headmaster phoning a pupil's house just to make sure that he wasn't playing truant.

Or maybe he was just curious to see what sort of man she could get.

'You're far too modest, Robert,' she said, half turning away from the dark figure towering over them and linking her fingers through Robert's.

'At any rate,' Nick said smoothly, 'this music is not to be ignored. May I?' He held his hand out to her, requesting her to dance with him.

'I'd rather not, actually. I've only...um...just finished

eating and I'd really rather sit and let my food digest before I go anywhere near a dance floor. Anyway, won't your…party be missing you?'

'Oh, I'm sure my party can do without my scintillating company for a few minutes.' His eyes did a leisurely appraisal of her, managing to eliminate Robert totally from his line of vision. 'Would *you*,' he said, finally turning his attention to the other man, 'be able to do without your…girlfriend for the duration of a dance? I promise I will take very good care of her, make sure that I return her to you in one piece.'

'I think I might be able to spare her for a little while,' Robert said, following Nick's lead.

'Oh, for goodness' sake! Will both of you please stop talking over my head? I can make my own decisions!'

Nick raised his eyebrows in apparent offended surprise.

'Oh, go on, Luce. You know you want to dance, and we both know that there's no way you're going to get me anywhere near that dance floor. We can carry on our conversation later.'

Lord, the conversation! Lucy had almost managed to forget all about that. Torn between her natural instinct to firmly but politely ignore the man looming above her, who had now seen fit to lean forward, supporting himself with his two hands on the small circular table, and her dread that Robert had not yet accepted her statement that she was far from ready to commit to any proposal of marriage, Lucy stood up with a forced smile.

At least the jazz band was having the decency to be playing fast, upbeat numbers. She would have a quick dance, without even the need to make any conversation, and hopefully when she returned to the table Robert would have put her reply to his question into some kind of perspective.

With that in mind, she allowed herself to be led to the dance floor.

CHAPTER FOUR

THE pressure of Nick's hand on her elbow as he led her away from the table sent a shiver of dreaded excitement shooting through her and she half glanced over her shoulder to remind herself that Robert was her date and the sort of man she should be with.

'He will be fine,' Nick murmured, noting the direction of her gaze.

The promise of a quick, fast dance evaporated as the band began playing a slow tune and she found herself pulled against him and held in place by one large hand pressed into the limp groove of her back. She could smell the exotic undertones of whatever aftershave he was wearing, mingled with his natural masculine scent, and her nostrils flared slightly.

'Did you come here to spy on me?' Lucy asked tightly. The palms of her hands were resting lightly on his shoulders, as though she might take flight at any moment and he was prepared for the eventuality. As if sensing the inclination, he raised one hand to the back of her head so that she was nestling into the nape of his neck.

'Yes,' he said bluntly, not bothering to disguise the truth. He hadn't intended to. He had dutifully sat through his six o'clock meeting with his financial director, in fact had spent two solid hours going through the accounts of the Tradewinds, noting when profits had begun to decline, working out theories, and thinking with irritable regularity about his secretary and what she was doing with her mystery date.

'You did?' Lucy asked incredulously. 'Why?'

'Curiosity.' Nick shrugged. 'I wanted to meet this date of yours for myself and I knew that if I asked you to bring him along to one of our social functions you would have declined. Politely but decisively.'

'That's...that's despicable!' Lucy sought for an adequate expression of outrage.

'Yes, I suppose it is,' Nick agreed. 'But curiosity can be a very powerful lure.' He himself had not known how powerful until he had found himself hailing a cab to bring him to the restaurant.

'What were you curious about?' Lucy asked tightly. 'Did you think that I might have been lying? Making him up?'

'Now, why on earth would you think that I would imagine that?'

'Because I don't advertise my private life all around the office!' she snapped in self-defence.

Instead of answering, he pulled her even closer so that she could feel the hardness of his thighs pressed against her. His dancing, she thought wildly, was positively indecent. She tried to manoeuvre herself so that she could see what Robert was up to, guiltily aware that, whatever prim outrage she was expressing, her body was reacting in quite a different manner to the man she was dancing with.

'Well, now you're being ridiculous.' Nick could feel her itching to get away from him and back to the blanketed safety of her date, but aligned to that he could also feel her body, which was singing a completely different tune, and he felt a spurt of irrational satisfaction.

He had spent two years locked up in a debilitating

marriage, one in which the joy of sex had gradually been replaced by the dull acknowledgement that he had somehow become a man whose appetite was satisfied with loveless coupling. He and Gina had continued to share the same bed and their bodies had still met with a certain amount of physical need, but that had been it. For the last six months of their married life they had not made love at all. He had buried his normal red-blooded urges in his work, always intending to finish their marriage once and for all, never expecting the hand of fate to do the job on his behalf.

And since then he had thrown himself into the fast world of sophisticated women and physically satisfying but emotionally empty sex.

Except, he was discovering, most of the time the sex was not physically that satisfying. It sated him temporarily but still left him with a hollow suspicion that he had somehow missed something, something vital.

Only one instance sprang to mind when every pore in his body had been held in a trance, when lovemaking had fulfilled every nerve, muscle and fibre. That one time with the woman he was now holding. Or was that just an illusion?

He didn't know. He just knew that when she had mentioned going on a date, with that pink-cheeked embarrassment that spoke volumes about how serious it was, he had been fired up with an unrecognisable urgency to follow her.

'And has your curiosity been satisfied?' Lucy asked tartly.

'My curiosity will only be satisfied when I discover what it is that you see in him.'

'With all due respect, that's none of your business!'

'I only have your welfare at heart.'

'No, you don't, and don't imagine that you can fool me for an instant with that pious voice of yours. Don't forget,' she added drily, 'I see too much of you at work not to know how you operate.'

'And how is that?' He was enjoying this conversation. It made a change to be argued with even though he knew that he would eventually and inevitably win the argument. He barely noticed the slight pause as one slow number finished and moved seamlessly into another. And nor, he thought with another one of those spurts of satisfaction, had she.

'Pious is not the adjective that springs to mind,' Lucy commented, unable to resist a smile tug her lips as she tried to imagine Nick Constantinou being pious.

'What is?' he prompted.

His breath felt warm against her cheek and suddenly she was exquisitely conscious of his body beneath its expensive, cleverly tailored sheath. All hardness and muscle. She was also exquisitely conscious of her own and the fact that her dress was of such flimsy, stretchy fabric that it was almost as though she wasn't clothed at all.

'Hard-working,' she said, trying to reduce their conversation to the prosaic and wondering whether it was her imagination or whether he actually seemed to be actively pressing her body closer to his than was strictly necessary. She felt another pang of guilt that she was enjoying this. She should have broken off their far too intimate dance to rejoin Robert at the table.

'Anything else?' he asked softly, fully aware that he was flirting outrageously. He wanted to bury his mouth against that soft neck and only the inappropriateness of such an action managed to bring him to heel.

'Ambitious,' Lucy said seriously. 'Intelligent and ruthless when it comes to the crunch.'

'Ruthless?'

'That's right.'

'Anything else?'

'Anything like what?' she asked innocently and she could feel him grin wickedly against her neck. It sent shivers of awareness darting through her body like dangerous electric currents.

'Well,' Nick drawled, 'hard-working and ambitious. Not the most scintillating adjectives in the world, although I should be grateful that you did not tack *nice* on the end.'

'Because you're not.' She sneaked a glance through the crowd on the dance floor and spotted Robert nursing his drink, apparently in pleasant contemplation of what was going on around him. Robert was *nice*, she thought suddenly, looking away.

'OK, then, what about sexy?'

'What about it?'

He felt her flounder momentarily and this time his satisfied response was a piercing indication of what he wanted. What he really wanted. Her. He wanted to discover for himself whether their lovemaking had been as glorious as his hazy memory told him or whether it had been just his mind playing tricks on him. And, as she said, she knew him probably better than anyone else did. She certainly saw enough of him, in all his various moods. She would understand that a relationship was not on his agenda. Unlike the women he had dated, who always seemed to understand perfectly at the beginning when he told them that he was not interested in commitment, only to find themselves seduced by the possibility of changing his mind somewhere along the way.

'You failed to include that in your list of descriptions.'

'Robert...will be worried if I don't get back to the table,' Lucy muttered in confused panic. A fine film of perspiration broke out over her body.

'He's a big boy. Surely he can look after himself for a few minutes without having a nervous breakdown.'

'We need to get back,' she babbled on. 'You never told me, was the meeting with Bob productive? I... Did either of you manage to get hold of Rawlings?'

'What have you been telling him about me?' He ignored her desperate attempt to change the subject and instead folded himself closer to her, as if keen not to miss a word she might be saying.

'Telling him about you? I haven't been telling him anything about you!'

'No? Why did he say that I was the big, bad wolf who always got his girl to spend her free time working at the office?' Somehow he managed to invest the *big, bad wolf* part of his description with an image of wicked excitement.

'I told him that I was lucky to get away tonight because you wanted me to work late, that's all,' Lucy said faintly.

'He's an...what did you tell me that he did for a living?'

'He's an accountant.' Lucy didn't for a moment think that he had forgotten. Nick Constantinou never forgot anything. He was capable of delving into the vast resources of his memory and plucking out minuscule facts and figures that other people had relegated to oblivion.

'Ah, yes, of course.' Now that he had decided on his course of action, he was surprised to find himself feeling almost happy. Happier than he had felt for some time, in point of fact. Of course, there would be one or two details to take care of, one of which was waiting for him at his table, also nursing a drink. Perhaps he could introduce her to Robert... The thought made him smile. No, perhaps not. Marcia, whom he had met briefly two months ago at an intimate dinner party of fifty-odd people, which had been hosted by his girlfriend at the time, would demolish Robert in minutes. Still, at least there would be no tearful partings. This was his first date with her and nothing would be expected beyond dinner and fine wine. If she was disappointed with the outcome, then he would be charmingly apologetic.

It did not cross his mind for a second that Lucy would turn him down.

'As an accountant I am sure he appreciates the fact that you often work irregular hours.'

'Robert tries not to let his working life intrude on his private one,' Lucy explained. 'Which isn't to say that he doesn't put in long hours. He does. He just doesn't devote all his spare time to his job. He does just enough to warrant his bonuses, and he's very well settled in his work.' Lucy frowned to herself, thinking of all the good things Robert had to offer on a permanent basis.

'Admirable,' Nick said in a voice which managed to convey the opposite.

'Yes, I think so.' She pulled away as the band finished playing, determined not to find herself pressed against him for another number. 'Now, I think it's time I got back to my table. Who are you here with?'

'Oh, just a couple of old friends. By the way, what did I interrupt when I came to your table?'

'Nothing.'

'You were telling Robert that you were too sensible not to go away and think about what he had said.' With Robert within sight, Nick lightly rested his hand on

Lucy's arm, guiding her towards the table. In his mind's eye he could envisage their naked bodies together. He tried to remember what she had looked like, what she had felt like, that one time when she had thrown caution to the wind, but all he could remember was the feeling of fulfilment that had washed over him like a wave. The details had been forgotten and the challenge of discovering how accurate his memory was made his blood swirl with sudden, hot excitement.

'Well, I shall see you tomorrow.' Their table was within sight and she waved at Robert, half turning towards Nick with a smile of dismissal on her face. 'Thanks for the dance.'

But Nick did not appear in a desperate hurry to return to his table. He reasoned that Marcia would be fine for a few minutes longer in the company of his cousin. Stavros was nothing if not entertaining and Marcia was clearly in the mood to be entertained. She had been drinking steadily for two hours and would probably not have noticed his absence from the table.

'You did me a favour.' Robert rose from his chair so that he could pull Lucy's out for her. Always the perfect gentleman. 'Poor girl would have ended up with mangled feet. Care to join us for a drink?'

Nick glanced over his shoulder, wondering whether he might be pushing his luck if he stayed a little longer. He wanted to find out a bit more about this man, discover what it was that Lucy saw in him. More to the point, he needed to establish in his own mind that there was no competition there.

Now that he had established his course of action, he saw absolutely nothing wrong in pursuing his goal. All was fair in love and war and she wasn't a married woman.

Lucy, following his eyes, glimpsed through the crowds to the table he was searching out and immediately saw the stunning brunette laughing alongside a tall, dark-haired man who had a drink in his hand. So that was his old friend. Hardly old, she thought with a sudden pang of jealousy that was extinguished almost before it had time to lodge.

'I very much doubt Mr Constantinou will be able to do that, Robert.' Impulsively she took Robert's hand in hers, hardly aware that she was doing it, only aware of the brunette, who had spotted Nick, waving merrily at him through the crowds. 'His friends are waiting for him.'

'Shame. Still, it was nice to meet you, and hopefully the next time we meet it will be at a celebration...' Robert slid his eyes over to Lucy and Nick looked at the both of them narrowly. Celebration? What celebration? He would find out in the morning. That settled, he leaned over their table, making deliberately sure that his arm brushed hers in passing,

'Now, you look after this young lady and make sure that she's fit for work tomorrow.' He glanced sideways, his dark eyes tangling with hers. 'I don't want to have to cope with any hangovers.'

'You won't,' Lucy said with a bland smile in return.

No, he didn't think that he would. Lucy would never indulge in excessive drinking, so hangovers would never be a problem for her.

But when nine-thirty rolled round the following morning he edgily began to wonder whether he had underestimated his secretary. He had never known her to arrive this late. And she had looked absolutely fine when she had left the restaurant. He knew because he had watched her every single step of the way as she had allowed Robert to help her on with her jacket, then linked her arm through his as they weaved a path through the jumble of people.

Her call came through when he was about to dial her mobile phone himself.

'I'm sorry. I won't be coming in to work today, Nick.'

'You won't be coming in to work. And may I ask why not?' It was her first day off sick and he attempted to sound sympathetic but it was a struggle.

'I feel pretty awful. I think I've come down with something.'

He could well imagine what and the thought did not predispose him to feel a shred of compassion.

'You seemed well enough last night.'

'I did feel absolutely fine last night…'

'Just can't seem to drag yourself out of bed this morning, is that it?'

'That's right.'

He heard the note of relief in her voice and frowned in irritation. 'There are a couple of important things I need you to do here.'

'And I'll be in tomorrow.'

How to get around to what he really wanted to find out? Whether she was ill or whether a night of rampant passion had exhausted her to the point where she just couldn't face the trek in to work. There was only one way.

'Sure.' White limbs writhing on a rumpled bed, entwined with Robert's. He was probably there right now sending her little secret smiles of conspiracy that she had taken the day off to spend it with him. In bed. Making love. He gritted his teeth together. 'Just rest. Take some medicine and call me if you cannot make it in tomorrow.'

Saying all the right things. But instead of immediately getting hold of someone to cover for her he stood up, not bothering to sling on his jacket, and strode out of the office, only pausing to pay a fleeting visit to Personnel so that he could get the information he needed. Her address.

Her flat was easy enough to find, although the traffic in London turned the simple half-hour trip into an hour and a quarter of intensely frustrating crawl.

Once out of the city, though, he managed to clear the West End, and the traffic heading up towards north London was less dense. He could finally put his foot down on the accelerator and build up some speed.

If she was taking time off work to be with her lover then he wanted to catch her at it. No warning. Just the surprise of seeing him there, on her doorstep. No chance for Robert to hide or escape through the back door.

As it turned out, he was forced to announce his arrival because her flat was on the third floor of a Victorian house and entry was only possible through an intercom system.

'Nick here. Could you let me in?'

'Nick?' There was a fleeting silence during which he could half hear her surprised intake of breath. 'What on earth are you doing here?'

'Just let me in, Lucy. I won't be long.' There was no way she could argue with a flat command and he pushed open the door when she obediently pressed the buzzer, taking the steps two at a time until he could see her waiting for him at the door of her flat, with a pale blue bathrobe pulled tightly around her.

Why wasn't she dressed? It was the middle of the morning! He ran up the remaining stairs and paused in front of her, taking her in with one brief glance before letting his eyes drift to the small hallway behind her.

'What are you doing here?' She repeated the question, this time with a slight frown of puzzlement in her voice.

'Files.' He held out one hand and the convenient excuse he had brought with him.

'Couldn't this have waited until tomorrow?'

'You might not be in tomorrow. You might be worse, and there's no point asking anyone else to handle this. You have all the information. Perhaps I had better come in.' His hand snaked out to rest on the door, which, he couldn't fail to notice, had only been partially opened. Lucy had not expected him and she certainly did not want him to enter her flat. With grim determination he brought a little more pressure to bear on the door.

'I really don't feel very well, Nick...'

'And you might well be worse tomorrow, like I said. At any rate, you can take your time with these. And it might be helpful having someone around if you're not well. To fetch and carry.'

'To fetch and carry *what*?'

'Cups of tea.' He shrugged impatiently. 'Sandwiches. Bowls of soup.'

Lucy skitted a glance over her shoulder. The last thing she needed was Nick Constantinou in her flat, filling it with his domineering masculine presence. But he wasn't going to go away and she was in no mood to prolong the debate, dressed as she was in a bathrobe with absolutely nothing underneath.

'I'll take the files.'

'Wish I could just hand them over, but there are one or two things I need to go through with you.'

Lucy all but groaned in despair as he pushed back the door and swept past her into the flat, his quick, dark eyes darting around him, taking in the small dining and sitting room to the right and the spacious bathroom to the left, the door of which was slightly ajar. Thank God she had had the wit to close her bedroom door. It was her private space—and the thought of those shrewd eyes taking in the crumpled bed and her other personal belongings made her feel ill.

'I'll make you a quick cup of coffee,' she suggested, reluctantly shutting the door behind her and following him to the kitchen, which he proceeded to inspect in depth.

Nick swung round to look at her, his eyes narrowing. The bedroom door had been shut. Purposefully? he wondered.

'No, no. You sit and let me make the coffee.'

'You don't know where anything is.'

'I doubt I will need a map to find anything in here,' he commented drily. 'Whoever designed this flat could not have made a kitchen any smaller if they had tried.'

'It's perfectly fine for me!'

'How is it that you cannot afford anything better when you are paid so well?' he asked bluntly, and Lucy flushed, seeing the flat through his discriminating eyes. The kitchen was poky, with a small table, big enough for two at a push, squashed against one wall. The fridge was small enough to be virtually useless and the paint on the cupboards, as on the walls, was grimy and in dire need of a coat of paint.

'I'm saving up to buy a place of my own,' Lucy mumbled. Of course, there would be no need if she accepted Robert's proposal. He had already called her and, having clucked sympathetically down the line for a few minutes, gently asked her if she was remembering to give his offer some thought.

'Well, sit down. You are not well.' He felt an uncomfortable twinge of guilt that his words of commiseration were utterly meaningless in the face of his behaviour, namely showing up unannounced on her doorstep on the pretext of having to give her work to do when he knew full well that every single item of so-called pressing importance he had brought with him could happily wait.

'No...I...I'll just go and change into something...else. The coffee's in the cupboard, the milk's in the fridge and the kettle usually works, although it can be a little eccentric at times.'

She fled. This was the first time he had ever been to her flat and she didn't like it. It was as intensely and painfully disconcerting as it had been on the dance floor, when his arms had been wrapped around her and the heat from his body had seemed to fuse with hers.

She kept her robe on for as long as possible while she rummaged in a drawer for a pair of jeans and a T-shirt.

She would just have to get rid of him quickly—and not because she was feeling under the weather. In fact, she was too aware of him to feel ill. She would just flick through the files, take a few notes and show him to the door. It was her flat, after all, and if she told him to leave then what choice did he have?

She dressed quickly, and just as she opened her bedroom door she was alarmed to find Nick standing just the other side of it.

He had had to follow her, to get a glimpse of what she was concealing behind the closed bedroom door. He could feel her *frisson* of shock as he took two easy steps into the room, his eyes drawn to her breasts rising and falling as she breathed quickly in dismay.

'Please go back into the living room.' Her voice was muffled but imperious enough to halt him in his tracks.

When she turned around to look at him her cheeks were bright red.

'Now!'

Ignoring her order for him to leave, he strolled further into the room so that he could check all possible hiding places. There weren't many. The bedroom was only marginally bigger than the kitchen, with a double bed consuming most of the free space and what was left divided equally into battered dressing table and an ancient two-door wardrobe. There was just enough room for a small circular rug next to the bed and space sufficient to weave a path of sorts from one item of furniture to another.

'I'm already dressed and ready,' Lucy informed him through gritted teeth. 'So if you don't *mind*...'

'Of course.' He shot her a lazy smile and stuck his hands in his pockets. So small, so cute and so immensely flustered by his presence. He doubted Robert could do that to her, for all that she had said in the past about her attraction to nice, reliable, predictable, dull men.

He was waiting for her in the tiny living room when she emerged a few minutes later, her colour back to normal.

'You do look a bit peaky,' he commented, indicating her cup of coffee with one finger and waiting until she had perched herself on the sofa next to him.

He would have to take things slowly. No fast moves, no obvious indication of underhand motives. The dull dissatisfaction that had been plaguing him for the past eight months had lifted and now all he could feel was the tantalising thrill of the chase, a gut-deep craving to have her again.

'Right.' He leant towards the table to rest his cup on some free space, brushing her thigh with his in passing.

'The files. Just three of them, but the Rawlings one is the most urgent.'

'What was the outcome of your meeting yesterday?' Lucy asked, edging slightly away from him. She was finding it hard to focus. Had he been about to barge into her room? She had been in such a panicked frame of mind, having him invade the privacy of her small flat, that her thoughts had been whirling and it was quite possible that he had knocked and she just hadn't heard. And, in all fairness, he had not seemed the slightest bit disconcerted by her response. He certainly hadn't displayed any signs of being sexually aware of her.

Thank goodness, she thought, frowning at the papers in front of her and trying to ignore the chemistry emanating from the man sitting inches away from her.

'Tried phoning the damned man,' Nick grated, 'who was unavailable, as usual. But I did speak to his underling and, from what we gather, there seems to be certain discrepancies with the allocation of money. Business has been pretty healthy so where the hell is the money going?'

He reached for his cup and then sat back against the sofa so that he could watch her as she flicked through the pile of letters in the file.

'Embezzlement?'

'Distasteful thought but it very well could be.'

'What will you do about it?' With her elbows on her thighs, Lucy turned her head to look at him.

'Get proof and then have him sacked if that's the case.' His black eyes were brooding as they met hers and Lucy hurriedly looked away.

'So what do you want me to do?'

'We need to work on a letter that's cleverly phrased. Nothing threatening, but enough for Rawlings to know that we're on his back now and we're not going to get off until we have answers.' His eyes drifted to the vulnerable nape of her neck. With just the smallest of efforts he could have reached out and grasped it and drawn her against him so that he could taste the delicate contours of her face. Her T-shirt camouflaged the curve of her breasts but his imagination, he found, could easily supply the missing details. The thought of large, rosy nipples made him harden in dramatic response. God, he would have to drive back to his place once he left here and have a cold shower before he went back into the office.

'If he's embezzling money,' Nick continued, every word perfectly assured although his mind had taken flight and was basking in the giddy anticipation of cupping those breasts, licking them, feeling her writhe with pleasure, 'we do not want to frighten him away. We want to catch him with his hand in the till. Tell me your suggestions.'

She had a beautiful face, a face that had no need for thick make-up. It was expressive and artlessly transparent, and as he sat back and watched her concentrate on the problem he had posed he idly compared it to the faces of the women he had been seeing over the past few months. Not one of those would ever have dreamed of stepping foot out of the house without a full covering of warpaint and at least two would go nowhere near a pool if it entailed getting their faces wet.

'Well?'

'Well what?' Nick blinked and realised that she had been asking him something while he had been busy speculating.

'Haven't you been listening to a word I've just said?' Lucy snapped irritably. 'You've barged in here with armfuls of work, and the least you could do is pay some attention to me when I'm talking to you.' She scowled, knowing full well what had been going on in that beautiful head of his. Lingering memories of the brunette who had adorned his arm the night before, she thought sourly.

'Of course I've been listening,' he said irritably, impatient with himself for allowing her innate concentration to drift. He couldn't carry on for too long playing the waiting game, he decided. He would never get any work done! He dutifully and seriously discussed what she had been talking about, working his way through the letter she had outlined, approving of her ability to be tactful without losing a sense of urgency.

'The other two files are fairly straightforward,' Nick said eventually, 'and, in fact, there is no need to rush and work on either of them.' He stood up and flexed his powerful body. 'Will you be all right on your own? I could go and get you something to eat.' Regrettably he would be unable to join her, enticing though the prospect was. There were only so many meetings he could cancel without his people getting suspicious. Although…

'Oh, I'll be absolutely fine,' Lucy said quickly, firmly squashing even the remote possibility of Nick returning to her flat and this time to share a meal. 'I'll do this work and Robert is coming round at four this afternoon.'

Nick's eyes narrowed and he strolled towards the door, chewing on this little piece of information.

'Taking valuable time off work?' He gave a hearty chuckle, his back to her. 'Must be serious!'

'Oh, yes,' Lucy said spontaneously, frowning at the thought that Robert would resume his gentle persuasion in the direction he wanted to lead her. 'He's asked me to marry him.'

CHAPTER FIVE

NICK was waiting for her the following morning. In fact, he had been sitting in his office since six-thirty that morning and had managed to complete a staggeringly negligible amount of work. He had printed out reams of pressing e-mails and they stared accusingly from the corner of his desk.

She was in his head. He couldn't quite understand why but assumed that it was because she was the one to have been there when he had most needed someone. He had been shattered on the night of the funeral, torn apart by guilt, rage and regret for a wasted life, and drowning in the fickle arms of alcohol, and she had been the one to take him in, to provide the comfort he had desperately needed.

All the women who had followed in his futile search for some kind of fulfilment had only served to remind him of the emptiness of relationships.

Was that what was driving him now? Some crazy desire to recreate the solace he had found with her? Or had she simply become a challenge which had been lurking there for months and which he had only recently acknowledged?

It didn't matter.

He just knew that when she had informed him that Robert had proposed to her he had felt as if someone had punched him in the gut. And Nick Constantinou did not take kindly to being punched in the gut. What red-blooded man did?

He glanced at his watch and then tensed as he became aware of her opening the outer office door.

He had kept his interconnecting door closed, all the better to get his self-composure fully in place before he said what he had to say.

By the time she knocked on his door, he was ready.

'How are you feeling? Better?'

'Much better.' She smiled sheepishly. 'I thought I was coming down with some kind of bug, but I think I may just have had too much to drink the night before, hence the aching limbs and screaming headache. I'm not accustomed to alcohol.' She paused. 'Would you like me to bring you in some coffee? By the way, I've managed to go through all those files after all.' She took a few steps into his office and handed him the lot. 'Shall I fax the letter to Joe Rawlings or do you want me to e-mail it to him?'

'Yes, bring me in a cup of coffee. We'll discuss Rawlings when you come in.'

He watched, sitting back in his swivel chair, as she departed his office and wondered what her reaction was going to be to what he had to say. Then he smiled lazily. He had been thrown by her shocking news that Robert had proposed but had noticed that there was no engagement ring on her finger. He had spent a restless night trying to tie things up in his mind, and at least on this count he figured he had fitted all the pieces together.

He had proposed and she had told him that she would think about it, that she needed time. Hence his overheard remark about her being sensible. *He,* Nick figured, was keener on putting the gold band on her finger than *she* was. *He* hoped for a celebration; *she,* however, still hadn't made up her mind.

He was still smiling when she walked back into his

office a few minutes later, primed with her notepad and her most severely businesslike expression.

'Close the door, would you?'

'I thought,' Lucy said, sitting down and crossing her legs primly, 'I might begin work on the end-of-month accounts once I've done all the usual jobs. Also, on my way in, Ann in Accounts Receivable told me that two of her girls have gone down with flu and she's asked whether she can call a temp agency for them to send someone along to cover for a couple of days. I thought, though, that I might lend a hand down there if it's all right with you.'

'No.'

'I beg your pardon?'

'No, it is not all right with me.' He leaned forward, joining the tips of his fingers at his chin and regarded her for a few long, thoughtful moments.

'Oh.' Something about his focused silence made the hairs on the back of her neck stand uneasily on end, and she licked her lips nervously. 'May I ask why?'

'Because as of tomorrow you will not be here to lend a hand to anyone.'

The unexpectedness of his flat statement made her mouth drop open in surprise, and then she was besieged by frantic thoughts as she wondered what she had done or said to have warranted being sacked. Because that was what he was saying, wasn't it?

It suddenly occurred to her how much this job meant to her. She might have kidded herself that she could walk away from it without blinking an eye, but, faced with the reality of doing just that, she realised that she needed this stability. It wasn't just the pay. It was being with him, filling herself with his life force even though she knew that it was wrong and stupid.

'You're firing me,' Lucy said numbly. 'Can I ask why?'

Nick shot her a surprised look. 'Firing you? What on earth are you talking about?'

Relief washed over her like a tidal wave.

'I assumed… I thought…' she faltered.

'You assumed and thought wrong. I have no intention of firing you. Just the opposite. You are to accompany me on a one-week trip to the Tradewinds. If Rawlings wants to try and avoid me, then he is going to have a hard time of it when we show up on the doorstep tomorrow.' It hadn't taken Nick long to arrive at that plan. In fact, it had been staring him in the face. The Tradewinds needed sorting out on a face-to-face basis, and he needed to get her out of London, away from the possibility that she might be idiotic enough to accept that man's proposal when marrying him would do her no good at all. He had no idea how he knew that, he just did, and it had nothing to do with the fact that he wanted her in his bed.

'Tomorrow?' Lucy squeaked. 'But…'

'I know, I know. You think that there is no way that we could possibly get out there that quickly, but I have a number of connections. We will fly to Barbados and then we can reach the island by a combination of small plane and boat. It will be a long journey, granted, but…' he mused on the irony of what he was about to say next '…worth it.'

'Actually, I was more thinking that there's no way I can just up sticks and leave without a minute's notice.'

'You have a passport, do you not?'

'Yes, of course I do, but…'

'And it *is* only for one week. You can spend the rest of the morning briefing your stand-in. I have already had a word with Bob and filled him in on what I will be doing. Once you've done that, you are free to go and see to your packing.'

'But…I can't just take off…'

'Why not? I am sure Robert will understand. You have told me a number of times what an understanding man he is.'

'What about clothes?' Lucy asked faintly. She had never done anything so impulsive in her life before, even though it was not of her doing, strictly speaking. 'What sort of weather…?'

'Hot. Very hot. Take a couple of hours to go shopping and that is an order. You will need casual clothes only. No suits. It will be baking hot, so…shorts, T-shirts, halter-necks, that type of thing…' he flirted with images of her scantily clad '…and bikinis, of course. Apart from the three pools at the hotel, the beach is a short walk away from the hotel front.'

'But won't we be working all day?' Lucy asked helplessly.

'We will be working, naturally, but not every hour of every day. And there will be no formal meetings, so even when we are working you will be free to dress down. Now, why don't you finish up here and you can go and do your shopping? The tickets should be with us at the check-in desk tomorrow.' He told her what time she needed to be at the airport, what time they would be leaving. The rest he left to her imagination, and then he settled down to enjoy the remainder of his day in pleasurable anticipation of the week ahead.

While Lucy pelted her way through Kensington, half thrilled to be going on a little adventure to a beautiful island, even though she knew that it was work, and half terrified at the prospect of being in Nick's presence for a week without the helpful intrusions of telephones, computers and meetings.

By the time she got to her flat she had bought a shameful number of things, which she guiltily justified as due to her considering the short notice she had been given. Shorts, small, stretchy tops, some sandals and a couple of lightweight dresses that she could wear to any meetings.

Her suitcase, when packed, was admirably compact. Just sufficient to last the week. No falling into the trap of packing a change of outfit for every ten seconds of the day to find that only two were needed for the entire duration of the stay.

Nick, the following morning, was suitably impressed by her economical one suitcase.

'Very sensible,' he said, grinning. 'Most women would use that suitcase as a holdall for their make-up.' He enjoyed watching her bristle for a few seconds, leaning against the pillar with his suit carrier propped up next to him.

Even dressed down as he was, in khaki-coloured trousers and a short-sleeved shirt, he still exuded a frightening aura of powerful, expensive sexuality.

Alongside him, Lucy felt ill-dressed and naïvely unsophisticated in her simple, straight, light grey skirt and pale blue cotton top. Any one of his admiring females would have dressed for the part and would have been looking as ultra-casually elegant as he was.

He was still smiling indulgently at her as he led her to the first class check-in desk, where there was no queue and where they were treated with a subservience that bordered on fawning.

Then on to a special lounge, where Nick was impressively at ease while she tried hard not to appear too wide-eyed and gawking.

'Are we allowed to talk in here?' she half joked in a subdued voice. 'It's more deathly quiet than our local library.'

'Oh, we can talk,' Nick replied gravely, 'just so long as we keep it down. We wouldn't want to raise the dead, would we?' He looked over to where two middle-aged businessmen were happily sleeping, and Lucy, following his eyes, shared his joke and grinned.

Nick felt as if he was seeing a thousand intriguing facets of her for the very first time. The way she tilted her chin up in a manner that tried and failed to appear haughty, the way her mouth had a habit of parting to reveal a glimpse of her pearly front teeth, the way the little sprinkling of freckles across the bridge of her nose seemed to darken when she blushed.

'So was Robert all right with your leaving him behind at such short notice?' he asked the minute they were sitting on the plush, huge chairs.

'Why shouldn't he be?' Lucy asked a little testily. Did he think that she was one of those women who prepared a week's supply of food for their boyfriends and invited them to bring their ironing and dirty washing round whenever they wanted?

'No reason.' Nick left enough of a silence to hang between them to be ensured of her attentiveness when he next spoke. 'It's just that some men think that an engagement ring allows them to start calling the shots.' He made a show of glancing at her finger. 'Oh, you're not wearing an engagement ring!'

'No, I'm not.'

'Have you not bought it as yet?'

'No. I...'

Nick inclined his head to one side with a show of lively interest.

'I'm still thinking about it,' Lucy eventually admitted.

'Very wise,' Nick said solemnly, 'very sensible.' Then he laughed. 'I would not like to see my eminently efficient secretary quit so that she can retire from life and start having babies...'

'Oh, no. Robert...' Lucy paused, finding herself in a trap. Quitting work to start a family was precisely what Robert had in mind for her. 'We haven't discussed any of that as yet. Like I said, nothing has been finalised.'

'And have you told him about...?'

'About...?' Their eyes met and Lucy had a heady sensation of being pulled under by the sheer magnetic force of his dark stare. He raised his eyebrows in apparent surprise that she didn't seem to know what he was talking about.

'About us, naturally,' he inserted silkily.

'There *is* no us.'

'Well, perhaps I phrased it badly. I meant...have you told him that you and I slept together...?'

'Once!' A steady pulse seemed to beat inside her head.

'So...I take it nothing has been said...'

'There's no reason to...'

'Is he the jealous type?' Nick raised one eyebrow questioningly.

'No!'

'No, I suppose not, or else he might have kicked up a bit of a fuss at your spending one week on a tropical island with your boss...'

'I'm not *spending one week on a tropical island with you*!' Lucy denied hotly. 'You make it sound as if...as if...'

'As if…what?' He frowned in apparent bemusement as she became more entangled in the knots she had already created for herself.

'Well…it's not a holiday, is it? We're going there to work.' At last she managed to drag her eyes away from him but she was still intensely aware of his dark, hooded stare as he continued to watch her.

'Of course we are. The only reason I asked was because I am a great believer in trust.'

Lucy stole a sidelong look at the harsh lines of his face. His mood had changed. From his light-hearted teasing of a minute ago, she could see that he had closed the shutters and was broodingly contemplating dark thoughts that she couldn't begin to guess at.

But, she thought with dismay, he was probably thinking about his wife. He had opened the subject of her getting married and it must have brought a rush of memories flooding back, memories of his own marriage and the trust and love he had lost in one terrible freak accident.

While she floundered in her own miserable thoughts their flight was called and she was spared the agony of trying to find something suitably innocuous to say.

When he did finally take the conversational lead, they were on the plane, and he began to chat easily and casually with her about the various places he had visited over a period of years. She knew that he was well travelled but she hadn't known quite how well travelled. He seemed to have been everywhere and to have seen far more than the average fun-seeking tourist.

And she was a good listener. Normally on flights Nick slept. But her obvious interest in what he had to say kept him awake, and it was with a little start of surprise that he heard the announcement that they could fasten their seat belts in preparation for the landing.

'It's conversation,' he told her. 'Seems to cut the travel time in half.'

Lucy laughed. 'I wouldn't know. The last time I went abroad was years ago, and even then it was to the Med. Not exactly the longest flight in the world. I've never been further afield.' She paused and then confided, 'Dad was never a great believer in throwing money away on long-haul holidays.'

'Is that why you're always such a sensible little thing?' Nick asked, knowing that his indulgent reference to her stature would make her hackles rise. It would also, he thought, reassure her that his motives were entirely innocent, despite his leading conversation earlier on. He could have kicked himself for falling into the trap of talking about her boyfriend.

Dammit, he had brought her over here to forget about him! But something inside him compelled him to elicit everything he could about the nice, unadventurous, stunningly dull Robert, as he liked to think of him.

'I'm not sensible all of the time!' Lucy snapped obligingly, only realising that he had been pulling her leg when he shot her an amused, crooked smile, to which she responded with a sheepish smile of her own.

'Why are you so provocative?' she asked sternly and he laughed.

'I like to see you blush,' he admitted honestly. 'Even the freckles on your nose look outraged.' He lightly traced the bridge of her nose with one finger and her breath caught in her throat.

'That's wicked.' Her voice sounded shaky, at least to her own ears, and she hoped that he didn't notice.

'I'm a wicked man,' Nick murmured, which sent her pulses into further overdrive.

'In which case, I wonder why you didn't bring your date here with you to keep you company.'

'Date? What date?' The frown he gave her was one of genuine puzzlement.

'The leggy brunette who was waiting for you at your table when you bumped into Robert and me the other evening.'

'Ah. *That* date. Hardly seemed fair considering this is work and Marcia has an allergic reaction to work. Besides, my cousin and I took her out for a meal. Hardly what I would call a date. In fact, I should not think that I will be seeing that particular leggy brunette again.'

'Good heavens!' Lucy felt a treacherous rush of relief as they stood up to begin disembarking the luxurious plane. 'Don't tell me she had the audacity to make a nuisance of herself!' This was more like it, she thought. He went out with glamorous models and she watched in seemingly amused cynicism from the outside.

She bent to retrieve her handbag from where it had slipped in the foot well and straightened to find herself staring at the broad, muscular expanse of his chest.

'Actually,' he said softly, not moving an inch so that she was compelled to look up at him, 'I came to the conclusion that Marcia is not my type after all.'

'You surprise me,' Lucy said with a forced laugh and he continued to look at her with utter seriousness.

'I hope so.' Three small words that crashed through her consciousness like boulders of lead. He could read the wariness on her face and continued, smiling, 'I am a great believer in never being predictable.'

Which, Lucy thought, barely noticing the details of the airport, allowing herself to be whisked along, is why you make the most unsuitable man in the world. Because, dull though it seems, predictability is the essence of a peaceful life.

And peaceful lives are for people who have no sense of adventure, a little voice whispered into her ear, a voice which Lucy resolutely ignored.

If the first leg of the trip had been quick and smooth, the second leg proved to be anything but. The airport was pleasant enough, and it was exciting to be surrounded by people of a different nationality, speaking with a different accent, but their connecting plane was delayed, and when it arrived it was so incredibly small that Lucy couldn't help but experience a slight twinge of apprehension.

'Don't worry,' Nick instructed, placing a reassuring hand on the small of her back. 'We won't end up in the ocean surrounded by our luggage and a hundred hungry barracuda.'

'How do you know? It doesn't look as though it could walk the distance, never mind fly.'

He laughed, and in the gathering dusk glanced down at her fair head, fighting the urge to steady her nerves by wrapping his arms around her.

'Trust me,' he told her.

And, quite ludicrously, she did, even though, when pressed, he admitted that he knew not the first thing about flying and would be at a complete loss should the rickety plane begin to spiral downwards.

There was just something about his bulk that made a mockery of her fears.

He seemed to know precisely what to do, where to go, and his massive self-assurance meant that he was treated like royalty for the entire duration of their trip, right down to when they boarded the boat that would take them to the exclusive island which was the home of the Tradewinds Hotel.

It was dark by the time they eventually arrived. Too dark to appreciate the lush scenery, although there were enough strange noises to stir her imagination—the steady, rhythmic chirping of the crickets in the undergrowth, the occasional guttural sounds of the frogs and unidentifiable rustles as they covered the short walk from the car to the hotel that could have been any number of things.

And it was balmy, with the merest hint of a breeze blowing up from the sea, which was a black strip behind them as they approached the hotel. The coconut trees thickly lined the narrow road, and Lucy could not get enough of the view. Through the open window of the car she could hear the rustle of the leaves and see their dark silhouettes swaying gently.

'The sand is as white and as fine as powder,' Nick said from next to her, looking with amusement as she drank in the little she could see, 'the skies are bright blue and the sea is coral reefed so it is as calm and as blue as a swimming pool.'

Lucy reluctantly turned to look at him. 'And you prefer to live in London?'

'One can have a diet of paradise for only so long,' he told her wryly, 'then it loses its charm. At least for me. There's the hotel.'

It wasn't quite what she was expecting. In her head she'd had images of a standard hotel, large and imposing and shrieking grandeur.

What she saw, bright under the floodlights at the front, was a low, sprawling Colonial-style ranch house, its impressive frontage overrun with flowers, the colours of which promised to be even more extravagant in full sunshine than they appeared under the false lighting.

'It coils in an S shape,' he was explaining next to her, 'with gardens and pools within the inner areas. The restaurants are housed in separate thatched buildings towards the back. The intention behind this hotel was to create a feeling of a home away from home.'

'Some home,' Lucy commented, raising her eyebrows ironically. 'If my home ever resembles this I won't need to go anywhere on holiday.'

Nick smiled in reply.

'Are we expected?' she asked, as the car drew to a leisurely stop outside the entrance to the hotel.

'No. Working on the assumption that Rawlings may well have something to hide, I thought it best for us to surprise him with our little visit. That way there is no chance that anything could be accidentally misplaced.'

'So...'

'So...you and I are registered as Mr and Mrs Lewis and will be sharing one of the suites overlooking the beach.'

'What?'

'Little joke.' Still, he found the undiluted horror in her voice at his teasing piece of fiction a little irritating. Wanting her was beginning to have tentacles he had not predicted. Not only did he want to sleep with her for purely selfish reasons, but he also wanted her to want him. Not merely to be attracted to him but to crave him with a need that was greater than all logic and reason.

'Oh, right,' Lucy said weakly, 'very funny. Ha, ha.'

'You and I are business partners checking in for a week's relaxation in order to work on some confidential data. Hence the individual rooms. I've booked both under your surname. Of course, tomorrow the fiction will no longer be necessary.'

'Won't you be recognised?' Lucy whispered as their luggage was removed from the car and the porter who had appeared from out of the shadows asked them to follow him.

'I doubt it very much. I have only been here twice in the space of nearly two years, both times with Gina. The truth is that so many celebrities use this particular retreat, the staff are virtually trained to pay no attention to faces.'

It was true. They were checked in with a stunning absence of curiosity. Nick barely seemed to notice his surroundings, but Lucy was very much aware of everything around her and it was an effort not to gawp. This sort of grand-scale luxury was the sort of thing taken for granted by the rich and the famous, but really so utterly out of her reach that she was acutely conscious of her lowly status in comparison.

The floors were all wooden, but the wood was rich with age, and huge, soft chairs in pale wooden frames dotted the open area. Behind the man checking them in was an imposing piece of whitish driftwood shaped like a twisted statue and rising up from a squat ceramic pot topped with pebbles. Fans whirred overhead, ensuring a constant supply of cool air so that the doors and windows could all remain open throughout the day.

'We'll make our own way to our rooms,' Nick said, the minute the check-in was complete, and this statement was greeted with the faintest of nods.

'You want Rudolph here to at least point out the restaurants?' the man asked, and when Nick shook his head he grinned broadly, revealing even white teeth. 'Well, just follow the smell of the food. Mabel is the best cook on all these islands.'

'It's very quiet,' Lucy remarked, tripping along to keep pace with Nick, who strode ahead with their two bags, barely appearing to notice their weight.

He slowed and glanced at her. 'There really aren't thousands of rooms,' he explained, 'and the rooms are spacious enough and designed in such a way that privacy is guaranteed. Several actually lead out to their own private handmade rock pools if guests prefer to remain utterly on their own.'

They were walking along a broad veranda-style corridor, which was broken with small tables and clusters of wicker chairs and from which trailing flowers adorned the archways that led off to the rooms.

'Here we are.' He turned through one of the arches into a small circular sitting area off which two rooms led. 'Yours is that one.'

'And yours?'

'Right next door.' He opened the door to her room, allowing her to precede him, and then quietly shut it behind him.

The room was huge, to say the least, and very quiet, with just the background hum of the air-conditioning audible. The wooden floor was peppered with brightly coloured rugs and one side was fully occupied with a long sofa, the size of a single bed, and two chairs, positioned around a low square table. The bed itself was a four-poster, cleverly dressed with fine mosquito netting that lent it a dreamy, romantic look. Through an open door Lucy could glimpse a massive bathroom and changing room and from one side there were doors leading out to a small veranda, which was lit and promised blissful peace to read a book in one of the chairs or lying in the hammock.

'It's gorgeous, Nick.' She turned to him with a delighted smile and he grinned back at her. 'What does it feel like to actually *own* this place?'

The question, the openly wry and admiring look in her brown eyes, the smiling curve of her mouth, invited a light-hearted reply in return, but oddly Nick found himself considering her question with unexpected seriousness.

Either the heat was getting to his head or the change in scenery had scrambled his ingrained passion for privacy.

He looked at her thoughtfully and for such a long time that Lucy's smile faltered.

'You don't expect me to give you a serious answer, do you?' he drawled, leaning against the wall and crossing his feet at the ankles.

So tall, so dominant and so utterly compelling. Even more so, if that was possible, here in the tropics, where the olive tone of his skin and the fine film of perspiration made him exude a powerfully sexual aggressiveness that seemed to fill her nostrils.

She was shocked at the force of her physical response and camouflaged it under a light laugh.

'Of course I do!'

'In that case, I will tell you the truth. Owning this place is like owning all the other hotels. They are all luxurious, all the top of their range, and I feel absolutely nothing except the satisfaction I have of knowing that they are a profitable concern for me. They allow me to take risky adventures on the stock market and to invest in uncertainties, knowing that I cannot be financially ruined.' He pushed himself away from the wall and strolled towards the doors leading out to the veranda, which he flung open so that he could walk out into the night air. He stood against the wooden railings, hands shoved into his pockets, and breathed deeply.

'That sounds very cynical,' Lucy said from behind him and he turned around very slowly to look at her.

Against the brighter light of the room he could not see the details of her face, which was half shadowed. She was very still, though, and her eyes were on him. He could feel it.

'Does it?'

'You should be able to get so much enjoyment out of places like this...' She hesitated, wondering if it would hurt should she mention his wife. 'Surely when Gina was alive you must both have loved being in your hotels...this one...'

Bitter laughter rose like bile to his throat. 'You look hot. I hope you've brought sensible clothes with you. Cotton. Very cool against the skin. Do you want to have something to eat in one of the restaurants?'

'I'd rather just have a shower and hit the sack, actually.' Lucy smiled slightly, and even with the shadows playing on her face he could see the shy curve of her mouth. 'I think I'll get up very early tomorrow morning and have a walk around the grounds, if that's all right. I don't know when you want to start work but...'

'Explore. Take your time. I can call for you around ten.' So that settled that. But he felt no inclination to go. He wondered what she was wearing under the severe little skirt and the sensible top. Was she feeling as hot as he was? Was a trickle of perspiration zigzagging between her breasts? He idly wondered what it would be like to swim naked with her right now, in the darkness. They would have all the privacy they wanted.

With an inner groan of frustration he moved away from the railing, prepared to take his leave.

For the moment.

Because he would have her and slay his curiosity and, he thought with sudden, dry perceptiveness, their lovemaking would free her from the delusion that she should marry her boyfriend. He was so ill-suited to her as to be laughable.

He would, he thought, with a bit of imagination, be doing her a favour.

With that thought in his head, he left the room, in pleasant anticipation of what the week ahead would hold.

CHAPTER SIX

LUCY surfaced from sleep to the sound of knocking on her door. Polite but determined knocking that seemed oblivious to the fact that all she wanted to do was stuff herself under the crisp white linen and carry on sleeping.

The room was very dark. She had closed the wooden shutters the night before and had also drawn the floor-length terracotta curtains across so that there was no chance of even a sliver of light penetrating the room.

There was a moment of silence, then a further knock, and with a groan of acceptance she padded out of her gauze cocoon of mosquito netting towards the door.

'What's happened to your ambitious plans to go exploring?' a familiar dry voice asked as soon as she had pulled the door open. Her bleary eyes flew open and she slowly took in a fully dressed, bright-eyed and bushy-tailed Nick standing in front of her. He was wearing a loose shirt that hung open to reveal glimpses of his torso and a pair of green and cream bathing trunks. Under one arm was a rolled-up beach towel.

In an immediate gesture of dismayed self-consciousness, Lucy folded her arms and tried to sidle behind the door to conceal her state of virtual undress. One unappealing vest and a pair of extra-small boys' boxer shorts sporting a print of jolly smiling dinosaurs.

He wasn't having it. He gave the door a gentle push, forcing her to step aside so that he could engineer his way in.

Recently he seemed to have made a habit of intruding into her private space, Lucy thought sourly.

'I thought you said that you were going to be up with the lark so that you could scamper around the grounds and have a look at the beach.'

Lucy scowled. 'I doubt the lark has risen as yet,' she retorted, 'and I'd be grateful if you could do away with your habit of invading my space.'

'I thought you would have been up and out. In fact, I'm shocked to see that you're still in your room. I really only knocked on the off chance...'

Lucy had manoeuvred herself to the back of the room, where she was pressed against the wall, arms still folded across her breasts, the very picture of discomfort.

Nick, on the other hand, looked remarkably at ease as he pulled open the curtains, yanked up the shutters and announced without a hint of apology that it was a quarter to seven.

'The lark has been up for hours.' He turned to her with a grin. 'And this is the best time to have a swim. Which is what I intend to do now. Why don't you join me?'

'Join you?' Lucy's mouth dropped open. This was supposed to be a working situation, she thought wildly, not a one-week jaunt with a man who still managed to fill her head, however much she scoffed at her gullible stupidity.

'As in accompany me for a swim? The beach will be deserted at this hour.'

If that was supposed to persuade her then he was barking up the wrong tree.

'I can't,' she spluttered, wishing that she had eight hands instead of the two which were doing very little to conceal her vulnerably exposed body.

'Why not? Other more pressing plans?'

He had her cornered and he knew it. What other pressing plans could she possibly have here? Typing? Phone calls? Memos to answer? She couldn't even cough up an unexpected emergency requiring the dentist!

'Oh, it's just that...that I've only just woken up.' She gave him an apologetic smile. 'Takes me ages to get my act together in the mornings.'

'Really?' He looked at her with a show of puzzled disbelief. 'You must get up at five in the morning when you're in London, in that case, considering you're usually in to work by eight. Anyway, I am happy to wait.' He beamed patiently. 'Outside, of course.'

'I could meet you down there...'

'Nonsense.' He walked towards the door and pulled it open. 'I'll wait.'

All remnants of sleep were banished as Lucy sped around the bedroom, rummaging on the shelf to extract her black bikini and something suitably drab to wear over it. She had somehow imagined that swimming would be a few snatched minutes at the end of the evening after a long day hard at it, cooped up in the hotel conference room, poring over files and records.

The hotel, for starters, did not possess a conference room, and work, she was beginning to realise, was not going to be the conveniently consuming exercise she had previously imagined.

Nor, it would appear, were her dealings in Nick's company to be conducted with various hotel employees around as unknowing chaperons of her wayward imagination.

He obviously felt obliged to show her something of his hotel and its grounds and thought that he was doing her a kindness in the process. Doubtless her jibe the night before about him sounding cynical about his hotels had struck a chord somewhere. He had probably thought that, for the likes of her, being in these surroundings was a heady experience, and had decided to play tour guide to all those things he took for granted. She sincerely wished she had never opened her mouth.

Only when at the last minute she paused to glance at her reflection did she see that her bikini, modest as it was in colour, was far from modest in style. It was high-cut, revealing the shape of her thighs, and dipped well below her navel with two strings on either side, which, tied into bows, constituted a half-hearted attempt at ensuring the garment didn't unravel at the first hint of mobility.

It had looked adequate enough for the circumstances when she had picked it up from its hanger. Now it looked ridiculously sparing on coverage.

'Ready?' Nick's voice reminded her that he was still waiting outside, ready to do his gentlemanly show-the-secretary-round-the-resort bit, and she quickly pulled a flimsy short-sleeved blouse over her and grabbed one of the beach towels with which the bathroom cupboard was abundantly stocked.

'Have you brought some sun-block with you?' he asked as they walked away from the hotel in the direction of the beach.

'At *this* hour?'

'The sun over here is fierce, even early in the morning.'

'Well, I *want* to get a bit of a tan, actually, if I can.'

'Do you burn?' He glanced down at her and his eyes dipped lower to where her loose blouse beckoned a closer look at the soft, round breasts encased in their strip of black.

He definitely could not look too hard there, he thought wryly. Becoming aroused would be impossible to hide beneath his trunks. He dragged his eyes back to the dazzling scenery, a splash of greens and browns interspersed with the succulent high colours of tropical flowers and foliage. She was informing him that she tanned quite easily, considering, and was beginning to relax as she looked around her, trying and failing to hide her delight at everything they passed.

He was more than happy to oblige her in her progress towards relaxation. He had one week to do what he needed to do. There was no race. He told her about the hotel, the renovations that had been necessary when his company had bought it out from an ageing English couple who had maintained it for years as more or less a family-style place with the options of a few rooms for paying guests.

'How could they possibly bear to leave?' Lucy asked, gazing longingly at the strip of white sand which they were approaching.

'One half of the couple died and old Mr Cooper-James couldn't face the uphill task of running the place on his own. He was more than happy to leave and get back to England. I gave him an extraordinarily good price, enough for him to retire without any financial concerns to bother him in his old age. Can you smell the sea?'

Lucy inhaled and smiled. 'Clean and tangy. The opposite of what I usually smell at this hour in the morning when I'm heading for the underground.'

'I admit London has its own peculiar scent.'

'The scent of pollution,' she agreed, stopping when they reached the bank of swaying palm trees that fringed the border of the beach. 'This is the bluest water I have ever seen in my life. It's like a swimming pool!'

'Some of the most tranquil sea in the Caribbean.' His eyes lazily scanned the horizon before resting on her. 'And all ours at the moment.' He led the way along the beach until the hotel grounds were no longer in sight, and spread his towel on the sand, making sure not to look at her as she wandered up to where he had taken position, sitting on his towel with his knees up and his arms hanging lightly over them.

'What time…?'

'Do people start surfacing? Depends.' He shrugged off his shirt and lay back on his towel with his hands folded behind his head. 'Sometimes there are one or two who like to get an early start, but for the most part people come here to relax utterly and that usually doesn't involve early rising. There's no need for them to get out of bed until midday if they don't want to. Breakfast can be served at any time and anywhere you want it, including on the beach.' He turned slightly so that he was watching her as she carefully spread her own towel, noticeably making sure that there was sufficient space between them so that their bodies could not even accidentally brush against one another.

'What luxury.' Lucy sighed. 'I'm beginning to see what you mean by the sun. It's hardly possible that it can be hot at this hour in the morning.'

'Luckily for you, I have thought to bring some cream.' He fished into the top pocket of his shirt and extracted a tube of sun cream. Not for him. He had never worn any of the stuff in his life before and had only picked it up from the bathroom shelf as an afterthought before he had left his room earlier. He barely glanced in her direction as he handed her the tube.

'What time shall we think about starting work?' Lucy

asked as she rubbed the lotion onto her shoulders and over her face.

How could the woman even begin to contemplate work when she was out here, with the sun beating down and the gentle lapping of the turquoise sea only yards away? He felt a little spurt of irritation.

Was she thinking about Robert as well? he wondered. Work and her absent boyfriend with his pleasant dullness and uninspired life? Could Robert ever afford to bring her to a place like this? Not in a million years!

'As soon as we have had breakfast.' He propped himself up on one elbow and scrutinised her profile. 'Do you intend to keep your shirt on for the entire time that we're here on the beach? For a start, the sun may not feel too vicious at the moment, but its effect, even now, can still be damaging, and there is no way that you can rub the cream all over yourself with your shirt on.'

Lucy wanted to ask him if he credited her with any intelligence at all. Show the secretary around, she thought, and make sure to point out the obvious because she's never been to a place like this and won't have a clue about the simple measures she would have to take for self-protection. Wasn't he taking his laboured consideration and thoughtfulness a little too far?

She pulled off the shirt and, still sitting up, began to massage the lotion over her arms.

Nick watched through half-closed eyes. There was no way he could afford to stretch himself out on his towel now, he decided, not when the appealing bounce of her breasts as she creamed herself was sending his imagination into wild overdrive.

He couldn't remember ever feeling like this towards any woman in his life before. Was it because he had slept with her once and the memory of it—what he could remember, at any rate—was powerful enough to keep his interest levels at this fever pitch? Had that one-night stand forged some invisible bond that was pulling him towards her? Or maybe it was because she was unattainable, virtually engaged to a man who gave the word 'dull' a new meaning.

'Lie on your stomach,' he drawled, taking the tube of cream from her slippery fingers, 'and I'll put some of this stuff on your back.'

'That won't be necessary.' Their eyes met and Lucy gave him a polite smile of refusal.

'Why is that?' He squeezed some of the cream onto his hand and looked at her with a raised, enquiring eyebrow. 'You think that the sun will somehow manage not to go anywhere near your back?'

'I...'

'Lie down. You might as well, Lucy, or else you might find yourself stuck to your bed for the remainder of the week with sunburn. A very painful experience, so I understand. It can also,' he couldn't resist adding, 'lead eventually to skin cancer.'

'Is that right?'

'Absolutely,' he assured her gravely. 'Something one should not take lightly. Why do you think that every room in this hotel is supplied with sun-block cream? Most of our guests are fair and the fairer you are the more prone you will be to burning.'

He wasn't about to give up and with a clipped sigh of resignation Lucy flopped onto her stomach, her body as rigid as a board.

'Relax.' His big hands descended onto her bare back and he began massaging the cream onto her skin, simultaneously rolling his thumbs along the top of her spine until she could no longer fight the squirm of enjoyment.

He dribbled a bit more cream on her back and resumed his thorough massaging. With the sun on the side of her face and the soft, rhythmic lull of the sea rippling over the sprinkling of white pebbles left from when the tide came in, Lucy felt her body slacken.

'Now, we must not forget the legs.'

'I can manage that myself,' she said, her eyes closed, not stirring.

'Well, now that I have the cream…'

She felt the pressure of his hands as he started with the back of her calf and lingeringly moved upwards, up towards the back of her thigh, and she only gave a horrified squeak when his fingers stole delicately a few centimetres under the stretchy band of her bikini bottom. Then she hustled herself back into a sitting position, her face bright red.

It was, he conceded, a very revealing costume, despite its drab colour. He doubted she realised just how revealing, but when she was leaning forward like that most of her breasts were exposed. Only her nipples remained concealed. Lord, he needed to go for a swim right now.

'That should protect you,' he said briskly, standing up. 'I'm going in. Coming?'

'In a minute.' You should be ashamed of yourself, she told herself restlessly, getting turned on by someone sticking a bit of sun-block on your back. But her nerves still felt feathered with electric currents as she watched him stroll down to the water's edge and wade in until he could strike out and swim. He was a strong swimmer. He cut through the water until he was virtually by the reefs that protected the bay and beyond which the light blue of the sea turned a deeper, more ominous shade of navy.

Only then, with him safely out of bounds, did she head for the sea, marvelling at its warmth. No need to test the water cravenly before gritting her teeth and taking the plunge. She splashed around for a few minutes, one eye warily keeping a look-out, then lay on her back, face turned upwards to the sun, floating.

She barely heard him swiftly skimming the water towards her and shrieked as he pulled her under, hands on her waist. She surfaced, spluttering, to find him grinning at her, his hair wet and slicked back.

'Now, what did I tell you about being careful in the sun?' he admonished, wagging his finger at her while she tried to recover some of her composure. 'Worst place to get the sun is when you're in the sea, and the easiest way you can do that is by floating on your back and drifting off to sleep.'

'I was *not drifting off to sleep*!'

'Your eyes were closed.'

'So what?' She paddled away from him and he swam towards her, his brown body alarmingly visible under the transparently clear water. Every muscle in his body seemed to ripple with strength and virility when he swam.

'Why don't you swim out a bit further with me?' he invited lazily. 'There is a sliver of coral reef just out here and you can see some wonderful fish, even without the aid of a snorkel.'

'No, thanks. This is as far as I go. And I think we ought to be getting in now. I shall have to wash my hair and blow dry it before we get to work.'

'You're right.'

Lucy could feel his black eyes boring into her, turning

her breathing into laboriously shallow inhalations that left her out of breath.

'It would be too easy to stay out here and forget why we came in the first place.'

'Oh, I don't think so.' She swivelled round and began swimming back to shore. She could feel him cutting through the water alongside her, his movement as fluid as a dolphin's. As soon as she could touch sand she stood up and half-waded, half-paddled up to the sand.

'You mean,' he said, latching on to her throw-away remark as they walked towards their towels, 'you cannot envisage being relaxed enough in a situation like this to forget about work?'

'How can I relax when I'm…?' Lord, she had been on the verge of saying *when I'm with you?*

'When you are…?'

'…when I'm being paid to be here to do a job?' Lucy finished lamely. She was reaching out to take the towel from his proffered hand when she realised that he was looking at her, no, *staring* at her, at her breasts, and as her eyes drifted down she realised why. Her bikini, which had already proved itself to be nothing along the modest lines with which it had wooed her in the department store, had now achieved the added bonus of turning into the consistency of clingfilm the minute it was wet.

The already minuscule top revealed the very pronounced jut of her nipples, lovingly outlining the generously sized circles with their protruding peaks.

As Lucy met his amused eyes with her dismayed ones he shot her a crooked smile, tilting his head to one side.

'You look as though you are about to explode. Don't be embarrassed. I *have* seen women's nipples before.' He knew that his matter-of-fact observation would have her floundering even more and he was right. If she could have willed the ground to open up and swallow her whole, she would have. As it was, she remained in frozen embarrassment, clutching her shirt. God, but he wanted to reach out and brush one of those hard peaks with his finger, dip behind the second skin of her swimsuit until he could feel the throbbing bud pressed into the palm of his hand. He felt a rush of restless, adolescent urgency that had him wrapping his towel around his lower half.

'I don't believe I asked for that piece of information,' Lucy said icily. Her brain had finally caught up with the situation and she hustled herself into her shirt. 'And if you were any kind of a gentleman, you wouldn't have...have...'

'Stared?' He didn't want to let this conversation go as yet. He wanted to make her aware that, however much she reminded him that they were on this sun-kissed island on business, there was a sexual awareness at work. He would make her see that until it filled her head and all memories of London, the rat race and most of all Robert were forgotten.

'That's right.'

'I apologise,' Nick murmured seriously, his eyes never leaving her flushed face. 'You are absolutely right. Forgive me. I sometimes forget that you English do not believe in being outspoken.'

There was no answer to that one and Lucy had no intention of attempting to find one. Instead she marched off along the beach with the blood pounding furiously through her veins, vibrantly aware that he was following her every step of the way with his eyes and equally aware that she would not give him the slightest opportunity to get under her skin again.

Why had he said what he had? So that he could see her squirm? She certainly didn't believe his excuse about forgetting the culture differences between them. He was as sophisticated as it was possible to be and would never have made any kind of *faux pas* unless it was intentional.

The memory of those brilliant dark eyes casually gazing at her breasts, at the outline of her nipples, the thought that he had had the sheer gall to mention them burned in her head for the full two hours it took her to shower, wash her hair and eat the succulent breakfast she had ordered from Room Service.

It was nearly ten by the time she went across to the reception area and she was tautly aware that it was in her interests to squash any incipient signs of informality from drifting into their relationship. What they had was about business. What Nick did for pleasure never had and never would include her and for that she should be grateful. Especially, she thought belatedly, with Robert on the scene.

But there was no need to squash anything. He was waiting for her, standing by the desk with two of the employees, casually but smartly dressed and back to being the supreme businessman that he normally was.

He introduced her to the two men to whom he had been talking and informed her that one of the two offices at the back of the hotel had been vacated for their use.

'All the hotel records will be brought to us so that we can inspect them and wrap this thing up. As quickly as possible.' His eyes were gimlet-hard as they alighted on the men, who were nodding with enthusiastic compliance. 'I will want the accountant to be available as and when we decide we need him. And get me Rawlings.'

He nodded curtly to Lucy before heading off towards

the back of the reception area and she trotted along behind him.

'Close the door,' he commanded as soon as they were in the office. It was a compact square room, air-conditioned and very sophisticated in comparison to the understated, laid-back charm of the rest of the hotel. No concessions were made in this room for fastidious, fussy guests. Here efficiency was of the essence.

The attractive man of only hours before, whose flagrant masculinity had had her senses reeling, was no more. In his place was her boss, the man who moved quickly and efficiently through piles of work, barking out orders, expecting her to keep up with him, as she usually did.

It had gone one before either of them realised that they were hungry, and rather than eat in one of the restaurants they chose instead to have a platter of sandwiches brought to them, along with cold beverages.

Nick risked switching off the air-conditioning so that he could fling open the French doors that led out to one of the more secluded areas of the extensive gardens, wryly informing her that as soon as they were finished eating they would have to return to artificial cooling or else they would never be able to get any work done.

Lucy readily agreed. The air outside was too languorously fragrant for concentration. In fact, as they sat outside on one of the wooden benches randomly placed to take advantage of the shade provided by a mature tree laden with flowers, she could feel her ability to concentrate begin to ebb.

'So what do you think?' he asked, his long legs stretched out in front of him and crossed at the ankles.

'About what?' Immediately her advance-warning system leapt into gear, but when she stole a look at him it was to see him frowning into the distance.

'About those discrepancies in the accounts.'

'They seem pretty consistent,' Lucy said thoughtfully. 'Invoices paid but without any back-up paperwork for supplies that don't appear to have any proof of receipt.'

The sandwiches were exquisite, stuffed with salad and an array of cold meats and tuna that melted on the tongue. With some effort, she listened to Nick, following the swerving of his mind as he explored the various possibilities for fraud that were beginning to emerge after only a few short hours, her eyes half closing to shut out some of the glare of the midday sun.

'I hope you've applied some sun-block to your face,' he remarked, breaking into his own flow of thoughtful speculation.

Lucy inclined her head slightly in his direction but kept her eyes closed. 'I wish you'd stop acting as though you need to protect me. I'm old enough to take care of myself, Nick.'

Nick felt a muscle in his jaw begin to pulse and he opened his mouth to deny that he was doing any such thing, then closed it again. For some odd reason he *did* want to protect her, although he knew from the tone of her voice that she was hardly aware of how accurate her observation had been.

What next? he thought impatiently. 'It wouldn't do for you to have to retire ill to bed when we only have one week out here to sort everything out,' he said brusquely, and her eyes flickered open. She sat up, having realised that she had somehow flopped back onto the wooden bench.

'And I won't,' she retorted with equal brusqueness. 'I *did* apply some sun-block. I wouldn't dream of coming all the way over here and then promptly falling ill from sunburn.'

'Oh, good God, Lucy, there's no need to get angry because—'

'I'm not angry. I'm just setting your mind at rest.' She stood up, brushing her hand along the front of her thin cotton skirt, which had seemed appropriate for working. More formal than the Bermuda shorts that she had glimpsed everyone wearing, and more comfortable than long trousers, which would have been unbearable in the heat. As it was, her stretchy shirt was already beginning to cling to her like glue.

'I see what you mean about needing the air-conditioning to work in,' she said lightly, aiming to defuse the sudden atmosphere that had sprung up between them.

'Without air-conditioning we would have melted an hour ago.' He shot her a smile that indicated a truce. 'And it seems hotter and stiller than I remember.'

Lucy looked at the flawlessly blue sky. Not a breath of wind was blowing. 'So,' she said, 'what next?'

'On with the accounts, and I think it's time we got the accountant in.'

Their food was cleared away with the silent speed of highly trained staff, barely interrupting their methodical progress through the stack of files that had been brought in and their full use of the computer to try and tally the increasing discrepancies.

By the time the accountant was called, Nick's single question was enough to make the man squirm with every semblance of misery.

'Mr Rawlings did a lot of the accounting,' he mumbled. 'He said that, as the manager, it was up to him to handle his fair share of the finances.'

Nick sat back in the chair and Lucy watched as he turned up the heat, firing questions until the man was visibly sweating.

Finally, at the end of two gruelling hours, during which Lucy had been taking notes, jotting down names of suppliers that didn't quite ring true, Nick leaned forward, resting his elbows on his thighs, and proceeded to subject the man to an intense scrutiny.

'And you didn't find it suspicious that your head office was making phone calls to you, asking questions which you patently should have been able to answer and yet could not?'

'Mr Rawlings always said that everything was fine, that he was in contact with you.'

Nick sighed heavily. 'How old are you, Peter?'

'Twenty-two, sir.'

'And you live at home with your family?'

'I'm married, sir!' He roused himself into an offended outburst that made Lucy want to smile, despite the gravity of the circumstances. 'I have a child. A boy. He is just over one.'

Nick held his head in his hands for a few silent moments. When he looked up his face was weary and drained of colour.

'So where do you live, Peter?'

'On the mainland. We have a small house. Matter of fact, I just got a mortgage from the bank.' His face creased into lines of worry. 'I need this job, Mr Constantinou, sir.'

'When are you expecting Rawlings to be back here, Peter?'

'Not sure, sir.' Peter looked hesitantly at Nick. 'He…'

'Spit it out.'

'He has family on one of the other islands near the

Bahamas. They say that there's a hurricane heading that way and he wanted to make sure that his family was going to be all right. If the hurricane comes, well, it could be one day, two...' he shrugged '...maybe even a week.'

'Hurricane? I haven't heard anything about a hurricane.'

'It's on the radio.'

'Right. OK, Peter, that's all for now.'

'Mr Constantinou, sir...' He stood up. If he had had a hat to wring, Lucy was convinced he would be wringing it now. As it was, he had to make do with his hands. 'My job...'

'Is safe for the moment.'

Lucy waited in silence for a few minutes after Peter had gone, then she broke it by saying,

'That was very big of you, Nick. Very compassionate.'

'What choice did I have?' He was still leaning forward, his chin propped on the palm of one hand, and he turned so that he was facing her. 'He looks as though he only just recently started shaving and he has a child to support.' He raked his fingers through his hair and stood up so that he could expend some of his energy by circling the small room, his head down-bent, his mouth set in a grim line.

'Can you tell me—' he turned to her, although he didn't look as though he was focusing on her at all, more on some hazy point in the distance, some place where his thoughts were preoccupied with matters far removed from her '—why the hell it is that people have children when they are virtually children themselves?'

'Well, I suppose...'

'A mortgage, a child! Good lord!' He paused and

stared out of the French windows to the stunning lawns outside.

'Not everyone has their life planned out to the last detail,' Lucy said softly.

'You mean like me?' He smiled crookedly and without humour. 'And what if I told you that my greatest wish was to have a child of my own?' The bitter statement was out before he had time to think and he was paralysed for a few deathly seconds by the sheer horror of the revelation, then he pushed himself away from the doors and resumed his seat behind the black and chrome desk. 'The boy will have to stay. He may be guilty of being manipulated and appallingly naïve, but the blame for all this...mess...is with Rawlings, and I intend to have his hide as soon as he steps foot back into this hotel.'

The mention of wanting a baby, she noticed, had been brushed over. For a split-second he had revealed his vulnerability and she knew, instinctively, that it was a moment best left alone.

'*If* he steps foot back here,' Lucy said, picking up the strands of their business discussions. She looked down at the thick wad of notes she had taken over the past few hours. So much for any doubts that this was going to be a working week! There was enough here to keep her busy for days. 'Shall I get going on all of this? I'll get some more print-outs from the computer and re-check the files to see if we've missed anything.'

Nick nodded grimly. 'In the meantime I intend to go and listen to the radio and find out if there really is any hurricane bound for these parts. If there isn't, then you might find yourself on another plane with me tracking the AWOL Rawlings down.'

CHAPTER SEVEN

'WHAT do we do now?' Lucy looked nervously across to Nick and drew her knees up so that she could wrap her arms around her legs.

This was the first moment they had had alone for two hours during which they had been herding the hotel guests together in the largest of the dining rooms so that they could explain that the path of the hurricane had altered slightly. No chance of being caught up in the dangerous vortex of the eye, but every chance that the island would be buffeted by the tail.

'Not much else we *can* do but wait.' He raked his fingers through his hair and looked at her. 'You were good back there, very good.' Better than good, in fact, he thought to himself as he continued to watch the elfin face staring solemnly back at him. He had provided his alarmed guests with the skeletal details of what they might expect and had somehow managed to send their panic levels soaring. Lucy, on the other hand, had soothed them, played down their fears, moved through the thirty-odd guests with just the right mixture of reassurance and blunt reality. Even though she herself had no real idea of what to expect.

'I suppose we should be grateful that it is now seven in the morning and we at least had a good night.' He stood up and moved to where the small figure was huddled on the big, brightly covered sofa, then he sat down next to her. 'Scared? Or is that a stupid question?'

'I've never been in a hurricane before.'

'And you won't be in one now,' Nick assured her. 'If the meteorologists are correct, all we should experience are some high winds and a lot of rain.'

'Just a little localised flooding,' Lucy joked weakly, and he felt a driving urge to gather her up in his arms and bury her against his chest. Women who collapsed in a crisis, he suddenly thought, weren't endearing. They were a nuisance. Lucy was plucky. Plucky and, dressed as she was now, in a pair of baggy, flimsy culottes and an oversized T-shirt, looking more like a wide-eyed, pretty boy than a woman who could drive him crazy.

He diverted his eyes to the windows behind her and the gathering blackness of the skies outside. It had dawned still but bright, and in the space of only an hour the sunshine had been eclipsed by racing clouds. Already the breeze was beginning to turn into more of a wind and the trees outside were swaying gracefully under its force.

'Are *you* scared?' Lucy asked him suddenly, and he looked at her with amusement.

'Now, do I look the sort of man who is afraid of anything?'

'Everyone is afraid of *something*.'

'Put it this way: battling with the elements does not frighten me, even though nature unleashed can be a terrifying force. What would be more terrifying than coping with this situation would be if one of those damn-fool guests started to panic. I have never seen a group of people more afraid than this lot. I don't think there was a single one who did not try and persuade us that trying to get them out in time would be the best solution.'

'I know.' Lucy looked at the strength in Nick's face and felt ridiculously content that she was here now, with him. She realised that she had not thought about Robert once, and with a sigh of recognition realised that, however nice he was and however secure life would be with him, she would have to finish their relationship the minute she got back to London. 'I can't believe that there were actually three men who complained about missing meetings if they found themselves cooped up here for longer than three days.'

'One can only assume that their wives do not possess the wherewithal to make them see that a few stolen days away from work could be worth their while.' He looked at her speculatively. 'Have you telephoned your boyfriend to let him know what is going on out here?'

Lucy flushed guiltily. 'Actually, no...it's been so...well, I've been so caught up with things...' It hadn't even occurred to her. Conclusive proof that Robert was not destined to be the man in her life.

'Well, perhaps you should,' Nick said casually, lowering his eyes and fighting to contain a smile of triumph. 'Just in case the lines go down. Unless, of course,' he added silkily, 'you are not too bothered whether he knows or not...'

Lucy leapt to her feet and went across to the telephone, turning her back to Nick while she dialled Robert's London number. In all events, she was spared a conversation, leaving her message on his answer-machine and assuring him that it was nothing to worry about.

'Not at home?' Nick asked conversationally. 'At this hour?' He glanced down at his watch. 'But it would be...well, very early in the morning, British time...' He watched her flush and raised his eyebrows in feigned surprise. 'Not out playing the field, is he?' he asked in a hearty voice, and her flush deepened.

'He sometimes spends the night at his mother's,' Lucy

eventually admitted. 'She...she lives quite close by and she's on her own. Apparently she's a little paranoid about safety and Robert feels duty-bound to stay over at her house every so often...'

'Odd arrangement.'

It hadn't seemed odd when Robert had explained this to her weeks ago. In fact, she had found it quite touching that he was such a devoted son. Now she realised that it was indeed an odd arrangement.

'He's very devoted,' she mumbled, and watched Nick's raised eyebrows lift a little higher.

'Sweet.' He stared at her, wondering whether to push the conversation further and decided that he would. The spectre of Robert having any claims over her ignited the devil in him. 'And what would be the arrangement should you two marry?' He realised that he was desperate to hear her admit that they weren't suited, that she had made a big mistake going out with him in the first place.

'I don't know,' Lucy said testily. 'Shouldn't we be going outside to see what's happening to our motley collection? Make sure they're not having nervous breakdowns?'

'He'd probably do the sensible thing.' Nick ignored her attempt to divert him from the subject and instead stroked his chin thoughtfully with one long finger.

'Which is...?'

'Oh, probably sell his house and get you to sell yours so that you can both move into somewhere big enough to accommodate his mother.' He allowed the appalling suggestion to sink in before shrugging dismissively. 'I have seen that arrangement before and my advice would be to avoid it at all costs. Mothers-in-law can prove to be difficult customers at close range, especially if their darling little boy is an only child...'

'Thank you for your advice.'

That wasn't good enough, Nick thought, his jaw hardening. 'In fact, you might want to ask yourself whether marriage to a man who still has not cut the apron strings is such a good prospect...'

Not only was he hell-bent on playing the good tour guide, Lucy thought suddenly, but he also considered her too inexperienced to know how to deal with a relationship! Could he be more patronising if he tried? She could have told him that she had already made her mind up about Robert, but perversely refused to give him the satisfaction of having him think that his little snippets of advice had managed to sway her.

'Oh, I think there's a big difference between a man who hasn't cut the apron strings and a man who is kind and thoughtful towards his parents,' Lucy said airily, heading towards the door and thereby indicating the end of their conversation.

She barely had time to turn the handle before feeling the curl of Nick's fingers around her forearm. 'I am not trying to pry into your private life,' he lied smoothly, 'I merely feel some responsibility towards you.'

'Why?' It was at times like this, when he closed the physical distance between them and she could feel the heat of his body, that her mind began going into crazy loops and her breathing became difficult. She had thought that going out with someone, shutting her eyes to Nick's inaccessible, idiotic attraction, would have got her priorities in order, and for a while Robert had been good for her. She had actually begun to think that with a little effort she could talk herself into obeying all her basic instincts for reasonable behaviour. It hadn't lasted.

But facing up to that still didn't make her stop hating herself for her stupid vulnerability.

'I suppose because you are not the world-weary, hardened type of woman who can handle—'

'Who can handle...what? Her emotions? A love life?'

'That's not what I meant at all,' Nick grated, wondering where he had managed to lose his control over their conversation. He was barely aware of the wind gusting against the windows, picking up leaves and debris and rattling them against the panes of glass.

'Look, I can take care of myself. Shall we just leave it at that and go outside so that we can see what's happening?' His dark face staring down at her was doing absolutely nothing for her peace of mind. She was just too aware of the proximity of his muscled body, which she had committed to memory months ago, on that one fateful night, and which yesterday's little jaunt at the beach had further imprinted in her head. She should push him away, but she had a sickening suspicion that if she laid her hand against his chest it would stay there and the little secret she had spent so long hiding would explode in both their faces like a bomb. She would just not be able to resist undoing the buttons of his shirt and running her hand over him so that she could touch his flat brown nipples, trace the outline of every sinew, dip down to touch the forbidden concealed in his trousers.

'You're right.' He released her and stepped back, pulling open the door and standing aside so that she could precede him. 'If we stay here much longer they will probably send a search party out to look for us.'

Now that his speech was over he was itching to get back to the situation in hand, she saw. With anyone else he would never have interfered, but she knew why he had chosen to air his opinions to her. However drunk he had been on that night they had made love with all the passion of his despair and her pent-up longing, and however much of a mistake it had been for him, he had not forgotten. A bond between them had been forged, even though neither of them acknowledged it, hence his misplaced sense of responsibility towards her. She could have wept. Instead she smiled brightly and edged past him towards the main area where they had earlier left the guests eating their hastily prepared breakfast and discussing their situation.

They found them exactly as they had left them and a quick head count indicated that not a single person had vacated the area.

As soon as they entered the room they were surrounded, and while Nick did his utmost to answer their barrage of questions Lucy allowed herself to be pulled to one side by two of the most elderly of their guests, sisters who had come to the island for a rest in the sunshine.

'It's picking up, isn't it, my dear?' one asked, while the other nodded sagely.

Lucy glanced over her shoulder and decided that it was infinitely better to deal with the Norton sisters than the predominantly brittle collection of wives who had gathered together to voice their complaints that their perfect holiday would be ruined by something as inconsiderate as the weather.

She was aware of Nick informing the men that they could make themselves useful by making sure that the windows to their bedrooms were secure and, for those whose rooms had private plunge pools, checking to see that there was nothing left that could be blown away and destroyed.

'Most of the staff are doing a last-minute check of the

grounds,' she heard him explaining in a voice that did not allow room for debate.

'All hands on deck, eh?' one of the men boomed, getting into the swing of things. 'Hear that, Mattie?' he broke off to inform his wife. 'Bit of a war-time situation here!'

'Hardly the same, dear,' she replied, which effectively led to a lively discussion of the privations of the war-time era. Preferable, Lucy smiled to herself, to the doom and gloom that had pervaded the room an hour earlier. She caught Nick's eye and he grinned back at her with mutual understanding.

He walked towards her and informed her that he would be going outside to lend a hand, checking to make sure that everything that wasn't nailed down had been dragged inside.

'You will be in good hands,' he informed the two old ladies, who were apparently not so old that their eyes couldn't twinkle at the sight of him.

'Of course we will, dear,' Gracie said, patting Lucy's hand. 'We're very lucky that you and your wife happened to be holidaying here. I think it's wonderful that you two can take time out from your busy lives to check out your hotels first hand. Don't you agree, Edie?' She beamed at her sister, who beamed at them all in return.

'Both such capable people,' Edie said. 'And might I say what an attractive couple you make?'

Lucy opened her mouth to protest and caught a warning glint in Nick's eye.

'I'll leave you for the moment, darling,' he murmured in a velvety voice, 'but don't worry, I'll be back before you know it.'

Lucy smiled faintly, excused herself from the two ladies and caught up with him on the way to the door.

'What are you playing at?' she demanded under her breath.

'I do not consider it diplomatic to let our guests know the reason we are here,' he hissed back. 'We get a fair amount of regulars coming here and any hint of a scandal, I assure you, would not do wonders for our trade.'

'But you could have said that I am just your secretary who's come over here on…on…'

'Ah, so you get the picture. If not on business, then what…? A passionate, undercover tryst?'

Lucy frantically thought back to what had been said to the group earlier. Not much, apart from the information that Nick owned a chain of exclusive hotels, of which this was one, and he had then moved on to discuss the hurricane, while she had stood alongside him, supporting his statements.

'So you mean that all these people here think… think…?'

'Probably,' he agreed drily. 'And I suggest we allow them to think that. The alternative, without them knowing the true reason we are here, is a seedy liaison.'

'But the staff know,' Lucy protested.

'And the staff here are trained enough never to indulge in personal conversation with the guests.' He could feel the stirrings of a plan in his head and a spurt of excitement raced through him like a sudden injection of adrenaline. 'Now, you go and chat to the old dears. I can see them peering over here at us,' he bent to murmur in her ear. 'They are of a generation that still believes in romance. Is that not uplifting in this day and age of sex without strings and relationships without commitment?'

'That's rich, coming from you,' Lucy gritted, but any further sarcasm was forestalled when he dipped his head lower to cover her mouth with his, pulling her towards him so that she could not struggle. God, but her lips tasted sweet. His tongue greedily explored the silky wetness of her mouth and he pulled her a little closer until he could feel the push of her breasts against his chest. When he drew back it was with great reluctance. 'See you later, darling.'

'I'll...'

'Be waiting for me?' he quipped, standing back, then he grinned again and vanished out of the door, leaving her trembling like a leaf.

Lucy had to plaster a smile to her face when she returned to the sisters and their benevolent approval of all things traditional. If they only knew the half of it! She weathered their politely inquisitive remarks, deflecting as much as she could with a semblance of shyness, and she was almost relieved when a sudden gust of wind uprooted one of the shrubs just outside the window and sent it hurtling away into the distance.

A little flutter of panic brought perspiration to her face. Nick had now been gone the better part of forty-five minutes and there was still no sight of him. What if something had happened out there? She felt sick at the thought of that, but the truth was that the landscape was changing into one that was hostile and threatening.

She moved towards one of the windows, as had a number of the guests, whose conversations had finally dwindled into silence, and stared at the black skies outside. It could have been nightfall rather than mid-morning.

'I hope your young man is all right, my dear,' Edie said, coming to stand next to her. 'I must say, I don't care for the look of this at all. It *is* going to be all right, isn't it?'

'Of course it is.' Lucy strained her eyes in every direction to see if there was any sign of Nick. The wind was now strong enough to force them to virtually shout if they wanted to be heard, and the coconut trees were no longer swaying gracefully, they were bending almost horizontally along the ground and seemed on the verge of uprooting themselves and taking flight. More plants were being pulled away from the ground.

'This is par for the course!' she shouted back to Edie. 'It seems very dramatic but it's nothing compared to what we would be experiencing if we were in the thick of things, I promise you!'

There was an ear-splitting crack of thunder and then lightning that illuminated the grounds for an instant, throwing everything into terrifying focus. Couples had found each other and several were clutching hands.

'Quite exciting really, Edie!' her sister shouted, and they nodded in appreciation of the elements raging outside. 'We old fools need something like this now and again to bring a little excitement into our lives!'

In the midst of this grand display of nature's supremacy, the rain began. Not a few polite drops, making way for the eventual downpour, but a savage lashing that made it almost impossible to see what was going on outside. And just when Lucy was beginning to contemplate going outside to see where the hell Nick could be the door was flung open and he strode in, soaking wet, unbuttoning his shirt, which clung to his body like an unpleasant second skin.

'She was worried sick about you, the poor thing!' Gracie bellowed as Nick approached them, his shirt fully off at this point.

'Were you, darling?'

'I just wondered where you were!'

'There's nothing more we can do now. We'll just have to sit it out. I'm going to change! Coming?' His dark eyes gleamed wickedly as rosy colour spread along her cheekbones.

'Of course she's going to come with you!' Edie cackled. 'Look at the state of her! White as a sheet!'

'I'd be better served here.' How on earth was she supposed to sound coolly contained when she had to shout just to make herself heard?

'OK!' In an intrusive and intimate gesture, against which she could do nothing without raising unwanted suspicions, he turned to stroke the side of her face before running his thumb along her mouth. 'Sure, now?'

'Sure!'

'All right! Now, tell me, sweetheart, where did you put my favourite pair of boxer shorts? You know the ones—black with red hearts.'

'Oh, I'm so sorry, *darling,* but that particular pair was shredded by the dog before we left England!' Which, her expression informed him, was precisely what she felt like doing to him.

'You'll have to buy me another pair, in that case!' He turned to the two old ladies with a smile of utter charm. 'She is such an incurable romantic! Loves to surprise me with little gestures to show how much she cares!'

This was taking it all too far, she thought helplessly. She could understand his reasoning about not wanting his guests to know why they were there. The hotel business was a notoriously fickle one, with new corners of the world opening up daily in an attempt to entice tourists, and he couldn't run the risk of his own hotel coming under any public scrutiny unnecessarily, but surely he didn't have to overdo the phoney husband-wife connection?

She knew that she was probably overreacting, and that he would run a mile if he had any idea how much his slightest look or touch or, worse, empty endearment sent her imagination into overdrive and just fuelled her own unwanted cravings. Still, it took a lot for her to banish thoughts of him from her head and instead concentrate on what was going on outside.

In the far-off distance, between the wildly cavorting coconut trees, the sea was just about visible, a churning mass of angry black water thundering against the sand, desperately trying to crawl up the beach and take its onslaught to the hotel.

It was eerily comforting when Nick returned to feel his arms around her shoulders; they were the very epitome of the loving couple as they stared out of the window together, mesmerised by the sheer power of the wind and rain.

In extreme situations, he informed her, violent spirals of air could lift cars and houses and certainly whip roofs off some of the less sturdily built dwellings. Lucy shivered and his arms tightened around her. Instead of objecting, however, she allowed herself to soften into his embrace, welcoming its warmth.

Lunch was a subdued business. The steady roaring of the wind made conversation sporadic and a fair number of the guests seemed reluctant to retire to their rooms, preferring the security of numbers.

In an attempt to alleviate the atmosphere, which had gone from panicked to plucky to depressingly aware that they were prisoners of a force over which they had no control and which showed no signs of abating, Lucy unearthed a cupboard full of games. Most were new, having been supplied to cater for children, who were not regular visitors to the resort.

'You go ahead,' Nick shouted when she showed him the selection. 'I'm going to catch up with some work.'

'Oh, no, you most certainly are not, my beloved little cabbage!' she yelled, to the delight of most of the guests, who seemed enamoured at the sight of young love. 'We can form into groups for those who want to play!' She distributed games and packs of cards. 'And you,' she said to him, 'can join Edie, Gracie and me in a game of Monopoly!'

'I hate board games!'

'Don't be such a spoilsport!' Lucy looked to her two companions for support and received it. Yes, it was a small triumph to see him cave in simply because he had no choice, given the lovey-dovey situation he had engendered, but it was a triumph well worth having, especially when it became apparent that he was on the road to losing.

'These dice are loaded against me!' he complained when he had landed on Park Lane, her property, for the fifth time in a row.

'I hope you're not going to be a sore loser!' She grinned, quietly pleased with herself. While the wind continued to howl outside, she had at least managed to divert the gathering gloom of the occupants. No one was moaning or imagining the worst. They were joining in with enthusiasm and, from the looks of it, most of them hadn't been near a game for decades.

She should have won. She had by far the most hotels. He should have lost comprehensively. As it turned out, she couldn't find out because there was a flash of brilliant lightning, the electricity went and the place was plunged into immediate darkness.

Amidst the sudden confusion, Nick clapped his hands loudly and announced that they would have to retire to their rooms. It was unlikely that the electricity would return in the foreseeable future. He knew, he said in a psychologically skilful manoeuvre, that he could depend on them to deal with the situation with the same level of cool-headedness with which they had dealt with the hurricane.

Several of the guests puffed themselves up with pride at the compliment.

He informed them that he would see to the staff, make sure that they were all OK, and then he, too, would be retiring to bed.

It was hard not to feel utterly safe with him in charge, Lucy thought dreamily, until she heard him say, in closing, 'And Lucy and I will be in the Toucan room! If any of you should feel alarmed during the night, for whatever reason, feel free to knock on our door!'

Her head snapped up in alarm and she leant forward in her chair, trying to decipher an expression on his face and failing miserably.

'Now, please remain here until I bring torches for everyone. No candles, please! And try to conserve the batteries in the torches, just in case…'

Just in case they were cooped up for another few nights? In which event, the cosily married couple would still be sharing the same harmonious marital chamber, ever alert to any alarmed guests?

She could feel her heart thumping by the time he reappeared with a handful of torches, distributing them and answering questions about when they could expect some of the weather to subside and how long before electricity would be reinstated.

By the time he got to her and flicked on their torch she had a whole host of questions of her own, none of which included anything to do with the hurricane.

'I've decided that Edie and Gracie can have the room next to ours,' he informed her. 'It has already been cleared out and prepared for them. I thought they would feel...safer...being a bit closer to us...'

On cue, the two ladies twittered their agreement and Lucy stifled a groan of impotent dismay.

'Cleared out?'

'Oh, yes, *cleared out.*' His voice was thick with meaning, and just in case she was still in the dark he draped his arm over her shoulder and whispered into her ear, 'Your things are now in my room. I told Maisie and Janette just to leave them on the bed. Thought you might want to sort them out yourself.'

'This is ridiculous!'

'Shh! Keep your voice down! Don't forget, we are the steady rocks. We have to maintain a united front.'

'But this wasn't the arrangement.' Lucy heaved a sigh that bordered on a sob.

'Nor was being struck by the tail-end of a hurricane,' Nick pointed out. 'Sometimes we just have to play things by ear.'

Gracie and Edie followed them to their new room, inspected it by torchlight, pronounced that they were satisfied and then thanked them for being thoughtful enough to know that they would have felt very nervous had they remained in their original rooms at the furthest end of the hotel complex.

'We chose them because we wanted peace and quiet!' Edie raised her voice to explain.

'Little did we know!'

Little indeed, Lucy thought grimly the minute she stepped into Nick's room, which mirrored the layout of her own.

'This is a farce!' She faced him belligerently with her

hands on her hips, but her aggressive stance was lost in the darkness, which was broken only by the limited circle of light radiating from the torch.

'What could I do?' He headed towards the bedroom, taking the torch with him, and Lucy followed, fuming, in his wake.

'You could have put them into a room closer to someone else!'

'They would not have felt as safe. They like you! They are old! Old and frightened, however chipper they appear to be!'

Lucy looked away and down to the king-sized bed with growing horror.

'And where am I going to sleep? Huh?'

'On the bed, of course. Where else would you expect to sleep? Here, you keep the torch so that you can put your stuff away. I'll have to leave the bathroom door open, though, so that I can see what I'm doing when I shower.'

'You can't *leave the door open*!' Lucy spluttered.

'How else will I get any light?' He turned away, oblivious to her simmering away in front of the bed, on which her clothes lay in neat bundles, and presently there was the sound of the shower, at which her mind reared up and she raced through the process of sticking her clothes in whatever free drawers she could find.

By the time he emerged with a towel around his waist everything had been disposed of and she was ready to take up her protests exactly where she had left them.

'And before you ask,' he told her, 'I have no intention of sleeping on a chair overnight. Like it or not, we are going to share this bed. I am going to open some of the small shutters in the bathroom and above the doors there so that we can have some kind of ventilation. Might be noisy with the sound of the rain, but if we don't we'll end up sweating. And we will have to sleep under the netting. Now, off you go with the torch and have your shower. By the time you get back I will be safely ensconced under the blanket and tucked away on one side so that there is no chance of our bodies touching.'

An impossibility, he acknowledged to himself without the slightest shred of doubt in his mind. There was no way he could lie in the same bed as this woman without touching her.

He was waiting for her when she finally emerged from the shower, wearing a long T-shirt. He could just discern her outline. He watched as she switched off the torch, placed it on the trunk at the bottom of the sprawling bed and edged her way to its side.

True to his word, he had left her a lot of space.

And, Lucy thought, he appeared to be asleep. She wasn't all that surprised. It wasn't that late but she felt exhausted. The day had been mentally stressful and it had been worse for him because, as owner of the hotel, he had had the full weight of responsibility land on his shoulders. He'd had to check the kitchens, the grounds, the staff, the food supplies, not to mention take on the task of soothing the ruffled feathers of his very expensive guests.

Mentally he must be drained.

She tentatively climbed into the bed, keeping herself as far removed from the gently breathing bulk to the left of her as she possibly could, letting the mosquito netting fall so that they were now in their own little cocoon.

When there was no sound from him she allowed herself the luxury of relaxing. After a few minutes she rolled from her cramped position, curled on the very edge of the bed, to a more comfortable one, lying half on her stomach.

He had opened the windows, as he had told her he would, and the room was cool even without the benefit of either fan or air-conditioning. And it was as noisy as he had told her it would be. The rain was like the sound of gunfire, battering against the windows and the walls, although the wind seemed less terrifyingly strong.

She could feel her eyelids begin to droop, and as she burrowed herself onto her side, curling into the blanket, the last thing she expected to hear was Nick asking her whether she was all right.

Her eyes flew open, and then he turned towards her and the bodies he had assured her wouldn't touch did exactly that.

Her knee, at right angles to her body, was straight against his thighs. Thighs that were not covered with anything. Lucy squeaked, and as her knee moved a few inches higher she felt something else, something that was similarly unclothed, something hard and erect and masculine and very much awake.

CHAPTER EIGHT

'I NEVER sleep in pyjamas.' It was the truth.

He wanted her. In fact, what he felt was bigger than want, it spilled into the realms of need. It was a force that had been building up inside him, he now realised, for months.

And everything had worked in his favour. He had planned to seduce her and events had seemed to lend his seduction a helping hand from every direction. The island, with its flavour of the exotic, the shimmering heat that slowed people down and gave them time to forget about the everyday pressures of trivial things that formed a wall between them. And then the hurricane. The hurricane, howling outside and gusting against the curtains so that they billowed frantically up. In a crisis, people were drawn to one another like magnets, seeking refuge with one another. What could have been more natural than that they should find one another? The fact that he had arranged for them to be sharing his quarters and his bed had been an act of providence because the old ladies really had not cared for the thought of being isolated on the other side of the hotel.

And she wanted him too. He had felt their attraction crackling like unseen electricity in the air, however much she tried to pretend that it wasn't there.

The problem was that now the stage was set he no longer wanted to seduce. He wanted to be the object of *her* seduction, he wanted her to admit her attraction to him, he wanted to hear her say it and feel her yield because she could do nothing else.

She had scrambled away from him like a terrified rabbit and he clicked his tongue in irritation at himself.

Lord, but it would be easy to move those crucial few inches that would make her escape impossible.

'You could have worn...*something*!' Lucy heard the nervous, panicked edge to her voice with dismay and took a few deep, steadying breaths.

'I could have,' he admitted.

'Then why didn't you?'

Nick propped himself up on his side, resting on one elbow, with the blankets draped haphazardly over his lower body.

'Because I wanted to make love to you.'

'You...*what*?' A warm, sweet sensation filled her body. She wriggled herself up into a sitting position and drew her knees into her body, with her baggy T-shirt pulled over her legs. She had to hug herself tightly to prevent herself from shaking.

The noise of the wind and the rain hurtling around them was like the distant roll of thunder.

'Don't tell me that you haven't guessed by now that I am attracted to you.'

'We're here on business!' She clung to that scrap of truth with tenacity. 'And...and you're *my boss*!'

'That didn't stop us once before.'

'That time was...was different!'

'Yes, and now I want to make love to you without the minor drawback of being under the influence of alcohol.' At least she hadn't tried to take flight as yet, but he knew that if he so much as edged a centimetre closer to her she would. Even if it meant sleeping in the bathroom.

'You...you *can't*.'

'Why not?'

'Because...because I'm not your type! We...we had this conversation before, do you remember? I'm not your type and the only reason you...well...is because there's no one else available...and, well...'

'You underestimate your powers of attraction.'

She heard the thick sincerity in his voice and drew her breath in sharply.

'And...and I already have a boyfriend.' Lucy weakly grasped the excuse and held on to it for dear life. He was attracted to her. She had spent so long wrapped up in her own crazy attraction to him that to hear him tell her that should have filled her with elation.

But she knew him too well. He might be attracted to her because they were far away from reality and the circumstances were, again, out of the ordinary, but, whether he admitted it or not, she wasn't his type any more now than she had been eight months ago when he had given her that speech in his office. She had seen his type close up. They were not small, boyishly built women with short hair and flat chests.

She had also seen how casually he discarded his women. After Gina, no woman had the ability to pin him down for longer than a few weeks, and that should be fine but she wasn't cut out for the one-night stand.

That was why she really should hold on to Robert's image. Even if *he* wasn't the one for her then another variation of him would come along sooner or later and, who knew, she might find Mr Right after all?

'No, you do not.'

'What do you mean? Of course I do! Robert—'

'You don't care about him. I doubt you are even attracted to him. You forget that I have seen you out together. You're like good friends.'

'Successful relationships are built around people being good friends!'

'You're going to fall backwards off this bed any minute. I assure you that I won't lay a finger on you, Lucy...unless, of course, you want me to...'

'Of course I don't want you to!'

'Are you so sure?'

There was a charged silence that stretched between them for a long time. Above the deafening sound of the elements raging outside, she seemed to hear the equally deafening sound of her own heart hammering inside her. And, try as she might, the shadows and angles of his torso whipped up a series of images in her head that was making the blood rush through her veins like acid.

'So if I touch your arm with my finger you are telling me that you won't want me to go further?' he asked with lazy, idle, utterly sexy speculation in his voice. 'Mm? You're telling me that you won't want to feel my finger trail along your collar-bone? That you won't want my mouth to touch yours? And then to—'

'I'm not listening!' She flattened her hands over her ears and squeezed her eyes tightly shut.

She felt the shift of his weight on the mattress and then his hands covered hers and he gently but very firmly pulled her hands down.

'Coward.'

Lucy opened her eyes and stared at him helplessly. 'I'm not the sort of girl who has one-night stands...'

'We've already *had* our one-night stand,' Nick pointed out. He brushed his thumb against her cheek and then stroked his fingers through her short hair. 'Even after only a few hours in the sun you're already beginning to go a golden colour,' he murmured. 'Would you tan naked on a beach for me, so that your whole body goes gold? No swimsuit lines anywhere?' He felt her tremble and had to restrain himself from plunging in. Instead he traced the outline of her slightly parted mouth, dipping his finger in, and with a little shock of piercing reaction Lucy closed her lips around it, drawing it in with a moan of surrender.

'Do you want me to leave you alone?' he whispered huskily. 'Do you want me to get into some boxer shorts and a T-shirt and occupy my half of the bed like a well-behaved gentleman?'

She held his hand and rubbed his damp finger between hers. 'I want you to...'

'To what? Get changed? Sleep on the sofa? On the bathroom floor? Make love to you for hours, grab a bit of sleep and then make love to you again?'

Lucy closed her eyes briefly. 'Yes. Yes, yes, *yes*. Make love to me, Nick. I want you to...'

Her words sang in his ears like a riot of sweet music. God, if she had told him to get dressed he would have had to fumble his way to the bathroom and have a very cold shower before he was fit to get back into the same bed as her.

He kissed her. A tender, deep, leisurely kiss, taking his time to explore the moistness of her mouth with his tongue, pushing her back against the pillows so that his heavy bulk was over her and she was running her fingers wildly down his spine. When he drew back from her mouth she gave a little whimper and arched up to kiss him again, her own mouth urgent with need.

'Do you remember the last time we made love, Lucy?' Nick whispered into her ear. 'I seem to recall that it felt…bloody wonderful…but I can't be sure. What was it like for you? Did you enjoy yourself then?'

'I enjoyed myself,' she said, meeting his glittering eyes and holding his stare. 'A lot.'

'Good.' He smiled slowly and then kissed her neck as he pushed the T-shirt up, steeling himself not to look at her breasts until the item of clothing was safely over her head and dispatched somewhere amidst the tangle of bedclothes.

Only then did he raise himself and pin her hands under his so that she was fully exposed to his roving eyes.

It was dark in the room, but not so dark, now that his eyes had adjusted, that he couldn't make out the swell of her breasts and the dark circles of her nipples.

For a woman who was not big-chested she had the most beautifully proportioned breasts he had ever seen, he decided. They were small but pertly rounded, and just looking at them sent an exquisite shudder of excitement rippling through his big body.

'Don't just look, Nick,' he heard her groan.

'What should I do, then, teacher?'

'Touch.'

'Like this?' He cupped them with his hands and gently massaged them, then rubbed the rough pads of his thumbs over the sensitised, erect buds until she was squirming under him.

'What next?'

'You know what I want!'

'I want to hear you give me instructions.'

'Does it turn you on?' she asked smokily, smiling, and he grinned back at her.

'Everything you say turns me on. You have beautiful breasts.'

'Then why don't you…?' She blushed furiously in the

dark at the thought of voicing what she wanted him to do with them.

'This…?' He stopped playing with them for only as long as it took for his mouth to replace his hands, and Lucy gave a deep moan of satisfaction as he devoted himself to exploring her nipples with his mouth and tongue.

Her hands had curled into his hair, and when she looked down it was to see his dark head moving against her chest, sucking at one breast while he caressed the other with his hand. It was a bombardment of sensation. She felt an insane desire to touch herself and was mortified at the shamelessness of the urge, but she needed to be touched down there. She was damp with wanting it and, as if aware of that, he kissed the flat planes of her stomach and then down to where the softness of skin was replaced by the cotton fabric of her underwear.

Instead of removing it, though, she was slightly shocked when he pressed his face there and breathed in deeply, pushing apart her legs and then kissing her most intimate region through the cotton.

It was an electrifyingly erotic gesture and one that made her close her eyes and raise herself instinctively up to meet his mouth.

Her briefs were damp by the time he tugged them down, allowing her the luxury of kicking them off the bed, and then, as he settled himself back between her legs, the actual feel of his tongue moving along the aching crease of her femininity was blindingly overpowering.

He placed his hands under her buttocks so that he could control his movements, and then took his time until Lucy wanted to cry out in sheer frustration.

'Now,' he said, breaking away when she was fast approaching the point of no return. 'Your turn.'

Lucy obeyed. It was glorious to finally be doing to this man what she had only ever imagined doing in her wildest dreams. She touched every inch of his muscled body and felt a sense of heady power when he shuddered beneath her. She licked his flat, brown nipples and rubbed her body provocatively over his until he was groaning.

Making love without the constraints that had been hanging over them the last time was a liberating experience. He made her feel reckless and gloriously wanton and she revelled in the feeling.

When, eventually, she slid on top of him he rolled them both over and captured her face with his hand.

'Next time,' he murmured. 'This time I need to be the one in control.' And as he thrust into her she felt every muscle and sinew in her body react with a surge of powerful urgency. She grasped his shoulders, then the small of his back, and felt him drive her to the soaring heights of fulfilment.

His manhood spilled into her and it was only when, spent, he rolled to his side and wrapped his arms around her that she realised that not once had he mentioned contraception.

Perhaps he thought that she must be on the Pill. Or maybe he didn't travel with a packet of condoms. More to the point, they had both succumbed to their own primitive urges that had left no room for rational thought.

'In case you were wondering,' she teased, 'I'm perfectly safe at the moment.'

'Safe?' he asked with drowsy bewilderment.

'My period only stopped a few days ago,' she elaborated, 'so there was no need for any protection.'

'Is that an invitation for more?' he teased, kissing her gently. He stroked her side and ran his hands along her thigh, revelling in the feel of her satin-smooth skin.

'Is it my imagination or does the rain seem to be lessening?'

They both listened intently for a few seconds. 'I think it's beginning to abate,' Nick said. 'I'll go and have a look.' He hoisted the mosquito netting over him and strode across to the windows, pulling back the shutters to look outside.

What little natural light there was illuminated his naked body, and on impulse Lucy followed him to where he was standing by the windows.

'Definitely on the wane,' he said, putting his arm around her, and she nestled against him. It was what she wanted to do but, even so, she felt a twinge of unease that these were stolen pleasures, valuable little windows of contentment that she would have to store up in her head for the inevitable rainy day.

'The wind's almost gone,' he said thoughtfully. 'We'll be able to begin picking up the pieces in the morning.' He looked down at her, at the silhouette of her naked body, and felt a rush of passion returning.

He had been right. Making love to this woman was as fulfilling as he had remembered from that one night they had spent together. His memory had not been as unreliable as he had thought. And there was no emptiness, no dawning suspicion that the act of making love had left him still searching for something elusive, that he had to leave so that he could clear his head.

'Fancy stepping outside?'

'Stepping outside?'

'Nowhere very adventurous. Just out of the French doors onto the patio. Feel the rain on our faces.'

'Isn't it dangerous?'

'Not any more. Nothing's blowing around any longer. By tomorrow morning the sun will be struggling to come out.'

'Well...'

He pushed open the French doors and Lucy stepped outside, instantly struck by the fact that, although it was still raining, the rain was warm against her skin and the air was balmy with the smell of the salty sea tangy in her nostrils.

It also felt wickedly pleasurable to be outside with nothing on. She felt him behind her and he wrapped his arms around her with his chin resting lightly on the crown of her head.

'If you look very hard,' he murmured, 'you can just about make out the silver strip of the sea. The beach will be littered with driftwood brought in on the tide.'

His eyes dipped down to see the rise and fall of her breasts as she breathed in and exhaled. Tenderly he cupped them with his hands, marvelling at how perfectly they fitted, as though they had somehow been fashioned for his big hands, then he stroked her stomach until his finger finally found a path to the soft, downy hair sheathing her femininity.

'We can go hunting for interesting bits of wood when the sun comes out,' he told her, while his finger continued its downward exploration until it was rubbing between the soft folds, finding the small bud and teasing it.

She should have been shocked. In truth, she had never done anything so public in her life before, even though there was no one around. The rain, now a steady, determined drizzle, washed over her like warm water from a shower and she could feel Nick's naked body slippery and wet behind her.

Everything around had a drowned, scattered look, but in truth, aside from the uprooting of quite a lot of the foliage, the damage appeared to have been slight considering the sound and fury of the elements earlier on.

'This hotel was originally designed in the knowledge that storms can sometimes strike,' he murmured, loving the way her honeyed warmth enfolded his finger and the way she quivered at his touch. 'Not much, aside from the plants, can be uprooted. All the outside furniture is firmly cemented down and partially made of wrought iron to make them heavier, more resistant to high winds. Feel good, sweetheart?'

'Mmm.' Lucy raised one leg so that her foot was propped against her knee and reached behind her with her hands to touch him. Then she swivelled to face him and continued to rhythmically stroke him while he did the same to her, two bodies gently being roused to a state of growing excitement.

'We'd better not return to the bed,' he said in an unsteady voice, 'not soaking wet as we are.'

'What are you suggesting?'

'Well, nothing that involves us lying on this hard patio or going back inside.' He grinned wickedly at her before lifting her off her feet, and then they were making love as she had never done before.

She was as light as he was powerful, and with her legs wrapped around him they had remarkably little difficulty in moving. In fact, it was doubly exciting to be making love outside, with the rain drenching them, his mouth finding her nipple as she moved on him, helped by the pressure of his hands around her.

They reached the pinnacle of fulfilment at the same

time and Lucy heard herself cry out with ecstasy before she subsided onto his shoulder and was carefully carried back into the bedroom and straight to the shower. From one lot of water to another, but then, dried and back in bed, so pleasurably satisfied that within minutes she was asleep.

She awoke the following morning to find that it was exactly as Nick had predicted. The debris from the hurricane had been left behind, and the sun was already staging a comeback. It filtered through the opened shutters, sending patterns of light through the room, and she drowsily felt one side of the bed to discover that it was empty.

For quite how long she had been on her own she had no idea.

All right, so they hadn't had a one-night stand. They had had a two-night stand, as he himself had pointed out.

She refused to feel remorseful. He had promised nothing and nothing was precisely what would be delivered, but she had *lived*. Magically and wholly for a few hours, and for that she was grateful.

The only question was: was she now to pretend that nothing had taken place?

She had no idea what to expect when she was finally dressed and heading towards the main restaurant in the hotel, where she was certain most of the other residents would have gathered in the aftermath of the hurricane.

She heard their voices before she even entered the room and she wasn't surprised to find that not one person had overslept. No longer were they guests who indulged themselves by staying in bed until the sun was fully up and half the day gone.

The only person who appeared to be missing was

Nick, and as she cast her eyes furtively around Gracie approached her and said, *sotto voce*, 'He's checking what damage has occurred outside, my dear.'

'I wasn't wondering—'

'Of course you were! I could see it in your eyes. He's been up for quite a while, actually. I know because when I looked out of my bedroom window at six this morning I saw him heading down towards the beach with a couple of the hotel staff. Amazing how quickly the weather can change over here, don't you agree, my dear? Just think—yesterday we all thought that the end had come and now just look outside…the sun's out and the rain is pretty much over. Marvellous. Shame the British weather can't follow the example. You should get yourself some breakfast, my dear. You look a little peaky. Sleepless night, was it?' Her pale blue eyes focused with eagle-like intensity on Lucy's face. 'Worried about us all, were you?'

'Now, Gracie, don't be naughty.' Edie had approached and was beaming cheerfully around her. 'Everyone's terribly excited to have been caught up in this hurricane,' she confided in a low voice. 'I've just been speaking to the Colonel over there and his wife. They'll be dining out on this story for years!'

Lucy grinned and glanced up to see Nick. And her heart skipped a beat. He was wearing a pair of khaki-coloured longish shorts and a cream polo shirt hung loosely outside. He looked expensive and fashionably elegant even though he was returning from a trek through the grounds, establishing damage.

She gave a tentative wave in his direction, feeling her courageous stance of *je ne regrette rien* beginning to fast evaporate and he nodded and moved across to where she was standing, stopping several times on the way to speak to various of the guests.

'What's the damage like?' Lucy asked brightly when he was finally standing next to her. It seemed ludicrous to be conducting this type of conversation when a few hours earlier they had been making love in the rain, and she could barely raise her eyes to meet his.

'Not as bad as it could have been.' He slung his arm casually over her shoulder and she wondered whether this was for the benefit of the sisters. 'Some of the people who live on the island have seen their crops washed away, though, and I've instructed the staff to start a programme of preparing meals to deliver for them until they can gather themselves together, and I'll also be making sure personally that financial help goes towards them re-establishing themselves.'

'My dear boy, that's wonderful!' Gracie clapped her hands in delight and Lucy felt her heart tug at what he had said. Was it any wonder that she had fallen so hopelessly in love with this highly unsuitable man?

'Now, how can we be of help?' Edie asked, whereupon there was general discussion about helping out with the distribution of food and maybe with some of the preparation so that members of staff could be released to be with their families.

'Of course,' Nick whispered into her ear as they watched the groups of guests gather to discuss details, 'they'll have to be supervised. I should think most of our guests haven't seen the inside of a kitchen recently, never mind actually prepared food in one.'

'Nick…about what happened last night…'

'Yes?'

'Well, let's just say that there's no need for you to put your arm over my shoulders.'

'But what would our guests think if I ignored you at a time like this? When we've just been through a potentially very dangerous situation?'

So that was it. What would the illustrious guests say? They were under the illusion that she and Nick were a blissfully married couple and how could he possibly disabuse them of that notion? The arm on her shoulders felt like a dead weight, something she should shrug off before she collapsed beneath it, but they were still surrounded by people; the show had to go on.

'Presumably, though, Gracie and Edie can now return to their original rooms…' Lucy volunteered tentatively.

Her heart took a further dive when he replied, without hesitation, 'Oh, I should think so. I'll instruct one of the staff to return their belongings to their rooms and to have your room cleaned and prepared…'

'Right. In that case I'll transfer my stuff as soon as possible.'

'Transfer your stuff? What are you talking about? You are staying with me from now on.'

'Staying with you?'

'Naturally. You didn't think that I could possibly be satisfied with just one night, did you? Are *you*?'

'Well…' Lucy faltered, daring to raise her eyes to his, and he smiled down at her.

'Well? Would you be satisfied with one night? Admit it, you would not. You still want me just as I still want you. In fact, I would like to take you right now, if it was at all conceivable that we could slip away and find ourselves a private corner somewhere on this island. I would like to spread a towel on the sand and make love to you with the sound of the sea only feet away and the sun washing down over our naked bodies…'

He had never meant anything more in his entire life.

He had vaguely believed at one point that sleeping with her would somehow get her out of his system, but once was not going to be enough.

All there was left to do was settle the small matter of Robert.

And when we return to England? she wanted to ask. Would his *wanting* still be as seductively powerful as it was here, a thousand miles away from reality? She had seen first hand how short his attention span was when it came to women, women with many more physical assets than she possessed. The plain truth was that he wanted for a short period of time and then, mysteriously, the wanting turned to boredom and indifference.

Because he had never recovered from his wife. No one could ever compete with a memory, least of all her, a woman in whom he had had not the slightest interest until now.

If she continued to sleep with him it would only be a matter of time before she saw his indifference reflected in his eyes, and when that happened not only would she be dismissed but her job would be on the line as well. He certainly wouldn't want to work alongside an ex-bed partner.

'I don't think it's a good idea if we continue with this…'

This was not what Nick had expected to hear. Her softly spoken words hit him like a physical blow in the gut and his hand tightened fractionally on her shoulder.

He wasn't going to let her get away. He couldn't. He forced himself to smile politely at some of the guests who were glancing across in their direction. In a minute they would have to move across to where plans were being made to help out. Their expensive guests appeared to be launching themselves into the spirit of charity work with admirable enthusiasm, including the high-level company directors who had previously been clamouring to escape the island in case they missed a few of their precious meetings. They could not physically leave the island just yet, and their energies needed to be directed into something, and helping out appeared to be filling the void.

They would need steering, though, and for that he and Lucy would have to be at hand. Good intentions and some spare time would not necessarily do the trick.

'We need to go and see what's happening with this lot,' he said grimly, releasing her from his hold only so that he could look down at her with darkly flaring intent stamped in his eyes. 'But do not consider this conversation finished.'

'Because it won't be finished until you get your own way?'

'How well you know me, my darling.'

Which meant what? Lucy wondered feverishly as the better part of the day was spent with her hands to the deck, preparing containers of food for the islanders who seemed to have suffered most, dispatching those few staff who were not outside already clearing debris to help deliver, making sure that the guests didn't overdo things.

She barely saw Nick. He himself was wrapped up in his assessment of damage and communicating with various transport services to establish when they could be reconnected to the mainland. Boats would be available the following day, but the light aircraft that normally ferried the hotel guests not for another three days at the earliest.

By six in the evening a fair amount had been accomplished. She had sent the guests away to relax and freshen up, though not before polishing their haloes with a few well-chosen words of praise for their efforts, and she herself was fully prepared to have an hour to herself—during which she would dredge up all the necessary common sense she could put her hands on, anything that would stop her from committing the ultimate folly of prolonging the tenuous relationship she had allowed Nick to instigate.

The last thing she was prepared for was to emerge from the shower with nothing but a towel wrapped around her, the bedroom door safely locked, only to find the French doors thrown open and Nick waiting outside for her, lounging against the doorframe, arms folded.

'I thought you might have locked the bedroom door,' he said lazily, 'which is why I took the precaution of making sure that I took the key to the French doors with me earlier on.'

Lucy was frozen to the spot.

'That's…that's…'

'Sly? Cunning? Underhand? All three, I admit.'

'I can't talk to you with a towel around me.'

'Why not?' He stepped forward and she held her ground, even though with every step closer that he took she could feel her carefully prepared high-principled, sensible speeches begin to unravel at the seams. 'Do you need to climb into a business suit to give you the strength you need to tell me that you don't want us to carry on?'

'I didn't bring any business suits,' Lucy said pedantically, while her heart continued to pound against her ribs and her eyes were drawn like magnets to his riveting face.

By the time he was standing in front of her, she could hardly breathe. He traced her skin along the top of the towel she was desperately clutching to her and she felt her breasts tingle in response.

'You want me and I want you. What could be simpler?' His eyes were hooded as he followed the feathery path his finger was making.

'Casual flings aren't my style, Nick.'

'That's not the song you were singing last night.'

'Last night I was—'

'Taking what you wanted and loving every minute of it. Life is too short for us to walk away from what gives us pleasure.'

'Speak for yourself,' she muttered unsteadily, and then gasped as his hand slipped beneath the parting in the towel and found one aching breast.

'Doesn't that feel good, Lucy? I know it does. Your nipple is hard.' This was hardly the subtle approach he had planned, but, God, he couldn't resist her. His voice was thick and shaky. He slipped his other hand beneath the towel, which dropped to the ground, exposing her in all her naked glory, and he groaned. 'For God's sake, Lucy, don't go for safety.' He dropped one hand to cup the soft mound between her legs and kept his hand there, exerting just the merest pressure.

The last of her coherent thoughts flitted out of her head and she raised her face to wordlessly offer her lips to his.

Robert was safety, and she had already decided that she could not possibly be with him.

Nor would she remain with this man, but to take these passing moments would be worth the heartache. He was right. To hell with safety.

'You'll finish with Robert when we get back to England,' he ordered softly and she groaned.

'I'll finish with him.'

A few days, a few weeks; maybe she could hold on to him for a few months. It was a gamble she was now prepared to take.

CHAPTER NINE

LUCY stared out of the kitchen window of her flat with her face cupped in her hands and a cup of tea, not a sip taken, resting on the small table next to her elbow.

It was raining. Not the hard, hot, pelting rain that she had seen six weeks ago when they had been caught up in the hurricane, but a typically English rain. Cold, fine, steady and never-ending.

Her flat bore all the tell-tale signs of a place that was rarely lived in. Three times a week, against Nick's wishes, she made sure to sleep in it.

'Let it go,' he had urged her more than once. 'It's a dump and it's inconvenient. Move in with me.'

She had weathered his anger and refused, even though the temptation to wake up each and every morning next to the man she deeply loved was as tempting as a long drink of water to someone dying of thirst.

The fact was that, realistic as she was, she was all too aware that the passion that still fired him up, and had them making wild, unrestrained love in the most inappropriate of places, was as transitory as a cloud in a summer sky. She had lasted the course far longer than any of the other women he had dated since his wife had died, but love was still a word that had never crossed his lips. Not once. Not even when his big body shuddered above hers, and in the throes of physical fulfilment he murmured words of wanting and needing.

She sighed and wondered what the hell he was going to say to the little bit of news she had for him.

He would be coming to collect her in half an hour and they were going to have lunch at a pub just outside London. Followed by the cinema for a romantic comedy for which he had expressed less than zero enthusiasm but which, he had informed her with a magnanimous, teasing smile, he would endure because she wanted to see it.

How easy it would be to read all the wrong signals into little gestures like that. How easy to think that perhaps, without even realising it, he really did love her—because would he put her interests ahead of his if he didn't? Would he have suggested that she move in with him if he didn't? Would he laugh at some of the things she said if he didn't? Would she turn in her chair at work to find him staring at her with that brooding, lazy expression that always made a shiver of suppressed excitement race down her spine?

But if he loved her he would have told her. Of that she was certain. He would also have been more forthcoming about himself because love was all about sharing and exchanging the information that mattered.

Oh, yes, he would talk to her about everything under the sun. Everything except his wife and their life together. The one time she had tried to raise the subject she had seen the shutters snap down over his eyes and just as easily he had changed it, leaving her in no doubt that any discussion in that area was not authorised and would not be tolerated.

And so what was going to happen now?

She idly began to sip the tea, wrapping both her hands around the mug, waiting for the knock on the door that would announce his arrival. He had had a key cut for the front door for himself, arrogantly telling her that he was a possessive man, and instead of being annoyed at such a Victorian concept she had blushed and felt a thrill of pleasure.

The knock came just as she was finishing her tea, and even though she was expecting him Lucy still felt her nerves jump at the prospect of telling him what she had to say.

She had dressed for the weather. Olive-green corduroy trousers and a clinging roll-neck long-sleeved T-shirt, over which she wore a cream and brown jumper that was cropped to the waist.

She had even noticed how subtly her dressing had begun to change. She still dressed sensibly, but far more fashionably, and twice on a Saturday they had gone shopping together, with Nick channelling her towards items of clothing that she would never have thought to wear, grumbling all the way that she should allow him to take her to upmarket designer shops so that they could do some proper shopping for her, instead of trawling the cheaper shops where she insisted on going.

'Snob,' she had teased him, and he had had the grace to redden, even though he'd denied it vigorously, informing her that she would be severely punished for thinking such an uncharitable thought. It had been another brilliant day. Her punishment had been to be made love to with such leisurely skill that she could still burn thinking about it two weeks later.

'I thought you would never open the door,' Nick growled, moving into the room to circle her in his arms. 'I spent all day thinking about you, you witch.' He kissed her mouth, taking his time, and then feathered her neck with little caresses. 'And why on earth have you dressed in the thickest jumper you could lay your hands on?'

'Because it's cold?'

'But won't it make it impossible for me to do anything with you in the back row of the cinema?'

Lucy laughed, distracted from her sombre frame of mind for a few minutes.

He, too, had dressed for the weather, and the dark colours made him appear even more rakish and devilishly good-looking than ever. Brute that he was, the tan he had acquired weeks previously had still not faded, while her trace of golden colouring was already a thing of the past.

'Only teenagers fumble with one another in back rows of cinemas,' she pointed out, pulling him into the room so that she could look at him fully, drink him in with her eyes.

'You make me feel like a teenager.' He had never felt so damned alive in his life before. Their night of passion on the island, which had had its dubious roots in his own burning curiosity, had not fizzled out into nothing, as he had half expected it to do. He had not grown bored and tired of her. Just the opposite. She was in his head all the time. It wouldn't last, of course, but for the moment she was as bewitching now as she had been from the very first.

'Is that good or bad?' She laughed, stooping to get her bag from the sofa, guiltily aware that the speech she had planned to make as soon as he walked through the door was already slipping away through lack of willpower.

'How hungry are you?'

'What?' He had a peculiar habit of jumping from one topic to another, without any link between the two. It was a characteristic that she was becoming accustomed to, although now and again he could still catch her sleeping.

'Hungry. Are you very hungry? This pub I have in mind is at least forty-five minutes' drive away, and that is not counting on any heavy traffic. Then another forty-five minutes to make it back to central London if we are to catch the movie in time.'

'I take it you have an alternative suggestion,' she said drily. Later, she thought. We'll talk later; we won't spoil this glorious Sunday, not yet…

'Well, by my calculations, if we eliminate the country pub…'

'But what about the best fish and chips I could ever hope to taste?'

'As I was saying, we eliminate the country pub and go to somewhere a little closer to the cinema, we then save ourselves at least an hour and a half, giving us more than ample time to…'

'To…?' The smouldering intent in his eyes left her in no doubt as to what he had in mind, but she allowed the excitement to build. At the back of her mind lurked the inevitable talk that they would have to have before the day was over, but, like a coward, she allowed herself to be swayed by him.

'What do *you* think?' he asked, pushing up her jumper, only to find the further restraint of her long-sleeved T-shirt. It took him only seconds to tug it out of the waistband of her trousers and then his hands were on her breasts. 'Mmm. No bra. You make a very good learner.' He caressed her bare breasts until every pore in her body was tingling.

How could she resist? How could she shut herself off sufficiently to give her brain time to function and her mouth the opportunity to say the things that needed to be said?

Making love with him was a taste of heaven. It was

shamefully easy to postpone unpleasantness, even for someone like her, someone who had never seen the benefits of trying to avoid the unavoidable, however gruesome it might be.

As it turned out, they made it to the cinema with only minutes to spare, by which time Lucy could barely concentrate on the light-hearted comedy. Her mind was busy catching up for lost time and she sat, huddled down in her seat, frowning and thinking, absent-mindedly linking Nick's fingers through hers.

And as soon as they walked out into the cinema foyer she turned to him and said flatly that they had to talk.

'Here?'

'No, not here. It's…it's too public.'

'It was a joke.'

'Oh, right.' She chewed nervously on her lower lip and looked at him. Lord, but he was beautiful. She was aware of the way other women looked at him, their eyes flicking sideways, running up and down the length of his body appreciatively. She wondered whether *she* had done that herself when he had been married, and even afterwards, when he had still been out of reach.

'What is the matter?' he asked, frowning.

'We just need…to talk. Perhaps we could go…'

'Back to my apartment?'

'No!' Not his apartment, and not her flat either. Nowhere where the temptation to touch him might get in the way of what she had to do.

'Yours, then.'

'No.'

'Well, I'm running out of suggestions here. It's too late and too cold to find an isolated bench in a park somewhere.'

'The office!'

Nick looked at her as though she had suddenly taken leave of her senses. 'You want to go to the office? Now? On a Sunday evening?'

'Yes.'

He shrugged and wondered what the hell could be so important that it had to be discussed in the office of all places. Perhaps she was going to talk to him about commitment, about settling down, and he wondered what he would say if she did.

Surprisingly, he felt none of the distaste that he had previously felt when some of his other women had broached the subject.

Maybe she wanted to move in but she had some conditions. He would listen to her and, dammit, he might even be tempted to meet her conditions. It was driving him crazy not having her by his side all the time. This morning he had woken up thinking about her, and he hadn't stopped until he had walked into her flat four hours later.

He had a gut feeling that marriage would be on the agenda. The word had not so much as surfaced since their affair had taken off, but Lucy would not want to be stuck on the outside for ever, and he needed her; lord, but he needed her. Her wit, her smile, the way she listened, the way she made love.

But did he need her enough to marry her? The memory of Gina and the hopes he had felt at the onset of their marriage rose to remind him of why he had vowed never to repeat the same mistake twice.

It was only when the taxi was pulling up in front of the building that he realised that they had completed the entire journey more or less in silence. A first for them.

When he looked at her it was to find her staring out of the window and playing idly with the thin gold chain she wore around her neck, a twenty-first birthday present from her godmother, who had died weeks after giving it to her.

'It won't be as bad as you imagine,' he said, stroking the side of her face with one finger, and she started.

'What?'

'Whatever is going through your mind…it cannot be that bad.'

'We're here.' She seemed to finally register that they had arrived at their destination. Now the office didn't seem like a good idea either. Not only was it the place where she had first slept with him, but they had made love there afterwards as well—three times, in fact. Once even when there were people around; he had simply locked the door and treated her to a fast, hard and blissfully satisfying twenty minutes.

But it was the least personal of the options.

'And there is no need for you to look as though you have arrived at the gates of hell.' He was tempted to hold her hand, but she had stuck them both into her coat pockets and was now lagging behind him, frowning, her head drooped in thought.

It occurred to him that she might not be thinking about moving in with him after all, or raising the delicate subject of a future together. It occurred to him that she might be thinking of doing just the opposite, might be thinking of breaking off their relationship altogether, and he felt a cold, poisonous trickle of apprehension curdle in his veins.

Her normally open, transparently clear face was closed and unreadable, and as they took the lift up to the directors' floor together he noticed that she hadn't moved automatically towards him, to nestle against him, but was standing stiffly by the panel with the buttons, hands still firmly tucked out of sight.

The floor was in complete darkness, and as they moved in silence along the corridor he flicked on various lights until the floor was bathed in bright artificial light.

'So,' he said, as soon as they were in his office and she was standing uncomfortably behind a chair while he went to sit on the sofa. 'What is this all about? No, allow me to guess. You want more out of this relationship than what we have, am I right? Though why we could not have discussed this somewhere a little more comfortable, I have no idea.'

'Nick, I…'

His fingers drummed methodically on his knee while he continued to stare at her, his clever mind trying to find answers on her face that were frustratingly unforthcoming.

'Come and sit next to me,' he said irritably, 'instead of standing there like a policewoman.'

She sat, but not next to him as instructed—instead in the normal chair she used for taking notes whenever she was in his office.

'Look, what I want to say…'

'I *did* ask you to move in with me,' he pointed out accusingly, darkly contemplating her avoidance of him. 'It is much, much more than I have done with any woman in the past.' He was losing the thread of this, he thought savagely, and he didn't know why. He just knew that whatever he was saying was flowing over her head.

'Yes, I appreciate this, but what I wanted to say…'

'You want to finish this, is that it?' What else could it be? It certainly wasn't a demand for marriage, at least not judging from her reaction to his feverish speculations.

He raked his fingers through his hair and stood up, glowering at her. He began to circle her, watching her down-bent head and getting more frustrated with every passing second.

'Well?' he prompted harshly. 'Is that what you are trying to tell me?' If it was, then he wasn't going to beg. In a complete turnaround to what he had been thinking earlier, he decided that he wasn't going to beg and cave in. She was just a woman, he raged inwardly, and there were plenty other women out there. She may have satisfied him, but if *she* could then so could someone else.

'Will you just let me say what I have to say?' Lucy blurted out. 'And stop walking round and round this chair! I need to see you!'

It was on the tip of his tongue to shout back that he was not going to take orders from her, but instead he remained angrily silent and resumed his position on the sofa.

'Well?'

'I'm pregnant.' Lucy held her breath and looked at him, not quite knowing what to make of the deafening silence that greeted her confession. It stretched painfully on until she found herself rambling into an explanation. 'I thought that I was in a safe period when we were…were out there…on the island, that I could go on the Pill as soon as we returned to England, and I did. I did go on the Pill. But it turns out that…that, well, I must have miscalculated. I couldn't believe it when I did the test two days ago, so I went to my doctor and he says…he said that sometimes it happens. You know, well, um, a woman's ovulation can alter, perhaps because of the change in time zones, I don't know…' Her voice trailed off miserably as she watched the expression on his face grow stonier.

What had she expected? Not this. Fury, perhaps. But she realised now, with spiralling dismay, that she had expected him to be pleased. She must have been mad! He looked anything *but* pleased, but that was what she had half hoped, in the depths of her, that he would have been. He had said, in one fleeting moment, that he had wanted a baby, hadn't he?

'So,' he said in a freezing voice, 'no different from the rest after all, were you, Lucy? When did you concoct this little scheme of yours? At what point did you decide that getting pregnant would be an easy way in to my bank balance? Was it that very first time we slept together? Here in this office? Me the worse for wear? Did you decide then? Did you think that you would bide your time, see if I eventually came for a second helping, so that you could then spring a little pregnancy on me?'

'What do you mean?' Her face drained of colour and she realised that she was shaking violently. She clasped her hands together and continued to stare at him in appalled fascination.

'You know exactly what I mean, you scheming little bitch. Tell me something, is this just *your* work, or is Robert involved as well? Ah, yes, I see it now. You and Robert planned this together, didn't you? You never made the mistake of going down the nagging route, dropping hints about commitment and wedding rings, *because you never wanted to get married to me anyway*. Your plan was simply to get pregnant and try and convince me that I was the father so that I could end up supporting you and your lover!'

'What are you talking about?' Shock at his accusations had turned her voice to a whisper, barely audible over the beating of her heart.

'Don't play the innocent with me!' He couldn't keep

sitting any longer. He had to move and he would have to try very hard not to get too close to the woman looking at him in such appealing and utterly deceitful bewilderment.

'I'm not—'

'Have you been running the two of us together at the same time?' The thought of that was so powerfully disgusting that he was paralysed for a few seconds into immobility. 'Of course you were. Or else you used the poor fool the same way you are trying to use me now. Used him to impregnate you so that you could come running to me, pretending that I was the father, expecting me to marry you or at least fund you for the rest of your life.'

'How can you say these things?'

'Because they are the truth!' His voice was like the crack of a whip.

'You're wrong. How could you think that of me? I haven't seen Robert since we got back to England! You know that!'

'How do I *know that*? We do not live in each other's pockets. You made very sure of that, made very sure that you kept a part of the week to yourself!'

'I didn't want...' Didn't want him to find her too pushy, she thought, fighting back the tears, hadn't wanted him to start feeling swamped by her until his passion curdled and he began to grow bored. At the back of her mind she had hoped that he might one day grow to love her. Fat chance, as it turned out, because if his reaction was anything to go by loving her had never been a possibility, not even a remote one. He was looking at her now as if she was a stranger, a stranger he despised.

'And even if you and your ex-lover were not in on

this together, that still left you, did it not? I was your passport to an affluent lifestyle and you decided to grab hold of it. Whichever way you look at it, you took me for a fool, and let me tell you something—no one, *but no one*, takes me for a fool!'

'I never took you for a fool.'

'No, you just overestimated your influence on me.' Her head was lowered and he didn't need to see her eyes to know that tears would be glistening on her lashes. Such a convincing picture of innocence, he thought harshly. Even now, repelled as he was by the manoeuvring that had finally brought them both to this point, there was still a corner of his heart that tugged at his emotions.

He went across to the window, through which the city looked like a nonsensical criss-cross of lights, and stared outside for a few seconds, then he turned slowly to face her with his arms folded, his expression grim and stamped with hostile distaste.

'Did you think that because I am a man of honour I would be willing to pay whatever price you demanded for another man's child?'

'Why do you keep suggesting that the baby isn't yours?' Lucy cried out. That, more than anything else, hurt. She placed her hand protectively over her still flat stomach.

Nick ignored the question. His eyes were flat and hard, like two jet stones boring into her.

'Or maybe you imagined that what I felt for you was love?' The word passed his lips and he felt a sickening rush of realisation. He had fallen in love with her. Every instinct told him to hate and he would listen to those instincts, but, dammit, she hadn't been just a satisfying sexual partner, or a satisfying woman to talk to, or someone who could make him laugh. It had all added up to something bigger and more powerful and he hadn't even had the wit to see that for himself until now.

'No, I—'

'Because if you imagined that then, by God, you were wrong!' He wanted to hurt her for hurting him and he hated himself for the pain he was enduring now. After all the messy business with Gina, the disillusionment, the lessons learnt, he was hurting now in a way he had never hurt before.

'I never loved you!' He made himself say it and watched as she flinched back from the statement as if from a physical blow. 'Yes, you and I were compatible in bed, but that was always as far as it went. The sex was good, I'll admit that, very good, but as for love...well...there is a yawning chasm between lust and love, is there not?'

'Yes, there is,' Lucy said in a dull voice. She finally got up the courage to meet his eyes without wincing. 'Well, now that I've said what I wanted to say, there's no point in being here any longer.' She stood up, looking around for her coat and her bag, while he continued to stand at the window, as implacable as a granite rock.

When he thought of her trekking back to that poky flat of hers on her own, a lonely little figure wrapped up in her thick coat, his heart constricted. He had to remind himself that in all probability she would be trekking back to Robert's house. Lonely she would not be. And, if not, then the conniving witch deserved her loneliness.

'I...when do you want me to clear my desk?'

'Now would be as good a time as any,' he stated bluntly.

'Now. Right.'

He followed her out to her office and lounged against

the door-frame, watching as she removed the few personal possessions stored in her desk.

'There's no need to hover over me, Nick.' She wanted to feel a healthy flare of anger but instead her voice emerged as weary and desolate. 'I won't make off with anything of any value.' She shoved her fountain pen into her coat pocket and a book which she had been reading two months ago and never finished. The plant would have to stay. Traipsing through London with a one-foot-high plant on the underground wasn't feasible.

'What shall I do about the things in your flat?' She had walked towards the door and now she paused, with her hand on the door knob.

'I will have them sent to you.'

'And my pay?'

'Now we get to the crux of it, don't we? Don't worry. I will not forget to let Personnel forward your pay packet to you, but if you imagine that you will be getting a penny over and beyond what you are owed by law then you can think again.'

This time some much-needed anger did come to her service and she lifted her chin proudly to look at him. 'I asked about my pay, Nick, because I'm going to need every penny I can get to support your baby when he or she is born. I realise you might not have wanted to be lumbered with fatherhood, but don't for a minute imagine that this baby is anyone's but yours. You can think up any reason you want to justify your behaviour, but you're lying to yourself. I never thought you were a coward, Nick, but you are if you're too scared to face up to your responsibilities.'

They stared at each other across the massive chasm that had opened up between them, and he was the first to break the silence.

'Get...out.'

'Goodbye, Nick.' She turned on her heel and exited the room, closing the door very quietly behind her.

It all felt like a nightmare. Had he really said all those things to her? Had he really accused her of the most vile, cold manipulations any human being could ever have been capable of? She very nearly thought that if she blinked hard enough she would somehow rouse herself to discover that it had all been in her head.

But it wasn't. She made it back to her flat in one piece and spent the remainder of the night in a state of muted shock, furiously trying to work out what happened next in the nightmarish play in which she now appeared to be the leading lady.

Telling her parents would have to come at some stage, and her mind reared up as she contemplated the disappointment she would have to endure, but the plain truth of the matter was that she would inevitably need their help. She just wouldn't be able to go it alone, especially not in London, where rents were high and children were not easily slotted into any kind of working lifestyle.

Which meant that she would have to leave London and go back to her parents' to stay.

Nor would she have the luxury of thinking things through. Time was not on her side. Fortunately, she had a fair amount of savings into which she could dip, but savings had a nasty habit of vanishing into thin air the minute they were dipped into and she couldn't afford to be out of work for too long.

It was only the following day, when she trekked down to the employment agency, that she was made aware of one small technical hitch to getting another well-paid temp job.

A reference. It was well within Nick's power to utterly

scupper any chances she had of getting work if his reference was detrimental.

She almost fainted when, having dialled his direct line at the office, she heard his voice fly down the end of the phone, straight into the core of her.

'It's me. Lucy. I…I'm phoning to find out whether you could provide me with a reference.' She held her breath and waited for him to either hang up or to tell her that he intended to do no such thing.

Nick could feel the tension oozing out of her, even though he couldn't see her face. He could hear it in her small voice. He could also feel a treacherous surge of elation at simply hearing her. God, but he was a fool!

'It's already been done,' he said brusquely. 'I dictated it at the same time as I informed Personnel to send you your pay packet. You need not worry that I'm going to concoct any lies about your working capabilities.' He heard her sigh of relief and he was tempted to ask her what kind of man Robert was if he demanded that she continue working even though she was now carrying his baby. He resisted. He had not had a minute's sleep for the entire night, thinking about the two of them, and he suspected that if the man's name so much as left his lips he would be back down that road of accusation and bitterness.

'Thank you.'

'Why thank me? You were a supremely efficient secretary.' He gave a harsh, humourless laugh. 'Some might say a little *too* efficient.'

'Please don't start on me again, Nick.'

'Your pay and your reference will be with you by tomorrow morning. Now, if that's all…' He let a few seconds elapse, furious with himself for his desperation to prolong the pointless conversation, then he let the receiver drop and sat back in his chair with his hands clasped behind his head.

Time was a great healer, he reminded himself. In a week's time he would find himself once again consumed by his work and functioning normally, and in a month's time he would probably not even be able to remember the definition of her face.

There would be no further reason for her to contact him again. She and her lover would be able to cope with the consequences of their ill-thought-out plans.

And he…he would simply move on.

He almost laughed with relief at the logical clarity of his thoughts. He picked up his address book and flicked through, but the blur of pages promised nothing. In time, he thought. Everything would return to normal.

CHAPTER TEN

THE choice of pub was not to Nick's liking. It was dark, smoky and packed to capacity. The bar was thick with an after-work crowd and the noise was reverberating. But it was appropriate.

He cradled his beer with both hands and then took a long swig before addressing the man sitting opposite him.

'Well? What have you got for me?'

'Same as I had for you last week, guv, and the week before and the week before that. Nothing.' The short, balding man flicked through the pages of his notebook. 'At least, nothing of any interest. Visit to the doctor. Once. Visits to the supermarket, several. Trips to the cinema. Three. All with other women. She's had two temp jobs, both in the Marble Arch area.'

'I am not interested in all of that.' Nick waved his hand dismissively. 'What about men? One in particular. Average height, medium colouring, average build.'

'No men of the average variety, guv. In fact, no men at all.' He shut his notebook, sat back and waited.

'Are you sure you are doing your job properly?'

'Look, I'm not about to complain at the dosh you're throwing my way to keep an eye on this lady of yours, but you're wasting your time. I've got a lot of experience in this field and I would have found out by now if there was anything going on. Nothing's going on.'

'Does she...look well?' He glowered at the private detective, daring him to show the slightest sign of amusement at the question, but Norman White maintained a perfectly straight face.

'Looks as well as is to be expected.'

'What is that supposed to mean?'

'Doesn't seem to eat much, least not on the occasions I've sat behind her at the restaurants she goes to with her girlfriends. Should be eating more, in her condition.'

Nick drummed his fingers impatiently on the small circular table and stared away into the distance. He had been a fool thinking that he could let this thing go. He had been confident that a few weeks would see him back to his usual routine, getting on with work and his social life. In fact, he was doing neither. He was pretty sure that, as far as outward appearances went, he was still running a tight ship, but his heart was no longer in his job. He went in to his office every morning, determined not to let her invade his head, and he returned home every night knowing that he had failed yet again.

'Think she might be planning on leaving London, though,' Norman said thoughtfully, and Nick's steady drumming on the table stilled.

'What did you say?'

'She's thinking of leaving London, going to stay with her parents. Overheard the conversation last Friday. Apparently thinks that London won't work for her and the kiddie when it comes along, and I tend to agree with her. Too fast, this place. My own daughter has a nice little place in Reading. Bit of countryside for the kids, no scrambling on the tube if you want to get anywhere.' He shook his head. 'Sooner she clears out, the better.'

'I do not recall asking you for your opinions, Mr White.' Leaving London. When? Tomorrow? Next week? Next month? Maybe she was already packing her bags and climbing into the taxi right now, on her way to God knew where. Somewhere far away from him.

A surge of panic rushed over him and he could feel himself perspiring slightly. 'Are you sure about this?'

''Less she changes her mind, but don't think that's going to happen, somehow.'

'When? When is this going to happen?'

'No date set. Least, not that I've been able to find out.'

'*Not that you've been able to find out?* Isn't that why I pay you, Mr White? To find out things I would not be able to find out for myself?'

'Look—' he drained his glass and declined the offer of another '—there's nothing more I can do. I'll take my week's pay and if you don't mind I'll call it a day on this.' He stood up and waited while Nick riffled through his wallet and extracted a wad of notes. 'My advice to you is that you sort out whatever problems you and this lady are having.' He inclined his head and stuck the wad of money into his pocket, keeping it all together with a thick rubber band. 'Good luck, and if you ever need me again, well, you have my card.'

Nick watched him weave his way towards the exit, then he sat back in the chair, frowning.

So Robert was no longer around. Even the most suspicious part of him could not foresee her concealing a partner in crime with enough cunning to fool an experienced private detective, especially considering that she would not have had the slightest idea that she was being followed.

She was on her own and she was leaving London, probably for good.

And it was time to make some decisions. He had wasted weeks having her spied on, which had proved what? It certainly hadn't sorted out *his* problem. He was still obsessed with her. Dammit. And what was going to happen when she left? Would she still be in his system?

He sighed and rubbed his eyes with his thumbs. She would always be in his system. Who had he been kidding when he had confidently assumed that out of sight was going to be out of mind? He still wanted to see her, hear her, talk to her, make love to her, even if she *had* betrayed him.

And that was the bitterest pill. The fact that he still wanted her with every ounce of his being, even though she had exploited him.

He wanted her and he had to speak with her. Before she left.

He thought of her flinging her few possessions in a bag, looking around the poky flat to make sure that she hadn't forgotten anything, while outside the taxi waited with its meter running. He pictured her locking the door behind her, sticking the key in an envelope and shoving the envelope under the door for the landlord to find. Lugging her cases down the stairs, panting and resting on every other stair because the pregnancy would make her tire quickly. Then driving away, to the station to catch a train that would take her out of his life for good.

He swallowed down the last of his beer, stood up, and then his feet were taking him outside, making him wait for a taxi, and every shred of pride that he had possessed disappeared as he heard himself giving her address, then sitting back and impatiently waiting for the car to take him to his destination.

He might have guessed that she wasn't going to be in when he arrived outside the converted Victorian house twenty-five minutes later, but now that he was finally here he had no intention of going. In fact, he hadn't felt so good since the whole mess had taken place weeks ago and he had slung her out of his office.

There was a coffee shop attached to the supermarket just by the underground. Nick bought himself a cappuccino, positioned himself on the most convenient stool at a long counter that faced the side-street, and waited.

He would wait until the cows came home.

He watched the ebb and flow of people hurrying into the tube station, and scurrying out of it. He had managed to make his way through three cappuccinos and was considering a fourth when he saw her emerge. She was carrying three bags and shifting them from one hand to the other, and she looked tired.

He left the coffee shop, hurrying outside and only slowing up when she was in front of him, then he began to gain speed from behind her. She wasn't even aware of him.

'You should not be carrying those bags in your condition.'

Lucy froze. Literally. To find the bags removed from her as her startled eyes took in Nick's broad, tall body as he stepped in front of her.

'What are you doing here?'

'These things weigh a ton. What the hell have you got in here?'

'Vegetables,' she babbled, barely blinking in case the vision in front of her vanished. 'It's cheaper to buy them at the market than... *What are you doing here?*'

'I need to talk to you.'

Memories of their last little *talk* sprang into her mind with disabling clarity and she flinched back.

'Haven't we done that already, Nick? May I have those bags back, please? I'm quite capable of making it to my flat with them in one piece.'

He ignored the request, instead falling into step with her until they were at the house, at which point she turned to him again.

'Look, Nick, you said everything you had to say the last time...the last time we were together. Now, just please go. Go and leave me alone. I'm getting on with my life and I don't want you coming here so that you can shout at me again.' *Getting on with her life! Getting on with existing would be closer to the truth.*

'I won't shout at you. I just want to talk.'

'What about?' Lucy asked antagonistically. She had stretched out her hand for her bags and he had ignored the gesture, until she clicked her tongue in irritation and stuck her key in the lock, letting him follow her up the stairs to her flat.

He could feel the hostility rippling off her in waves as he ascended the staircase in her wake. A month ago he would have been enraged at the thought that she could be hostile towards him when he had every reason to be the one dishing it out. Now things were different.

'So. You're here. Now, do you mind explaining what you want?' Lucy turned towards him with her hands on her hips and her lips drawn into a thin, straight line. The cold night breeze had ruffled her hair, giving her that tomboyish, elfin appearance that he loved with such maddening desperation.

'How are you?'

'I just told you, I'm fine.'

'And aren't you going to ask me how *I* am?'

'I don't *care* how you are.' She removed her hands from her hips and folded them mutinously across her chest. The man had a nerve. The last time they had been together he had battered every emotional defence she possessed and, not content with that little performance, here he was again, larger than life, prepared to dole out more of the same.

'Well, I am bloody awful, just in case you were a little bit curious.' His black eyes clashed with hers and he stood where he was, not moving an inch.

'Good. I have no doubt you deserve it.'

'You are not making this any easier for me.'

'In which case you're tasting some of your own medicine.' She gave a bitter little laugh that stuck in her throat and threatened to turn into a sob. A stupid, self-pitying sob. And there was no way she was going to give him the satisfaction of seeing that sort of response.

'You look too thin. You haven't been eating properly.'

'And since when is my health any of your business?' She couldn't face him. It was too much. She headed towards the kitchen, regretting the impulse the minute she was there because he had followed her in and dwarfed the small room with his presence. 'I'm nothing but a conniving gold-digger, after all, in cahoots with my lover.'

'I know you have not seen him since you returned to England.'

'What?'

'You heard me.' Nick sat down on one of the small wooden chairs and rested his elbows on the table.

'And how do you know that?' She tried to inject an element of scorn and indifference into her laugh, but it emerged as a bewildered croak.

'Because,' Nick said calmly, 'I have had you followed.'

'You *what*?'

'Why do you keep asking me to repeat what I have

said, when we both know that you heard perfectly well the first time around?'

'You *had me followed*? How *dare* you?'

Nick looked down at his long brown fingers. 'I needed to find out...'

'You needed to find out.' The tenor of her voice had dropped into the Arctic sphere. 'And would you mind telling me exactly what you needed to find out?'

'Whether you were still seeing that man.' Discomfort made his face darken.

'By *that* man I take it you mean Robert? My fellow con-man? And why would it have made a difference whether I had been seeing him or not? Surely it wouldn't have mattered to you, since you had managed to expose our evil little plan.'

'Have you any idea what it took for me to come here?' Nick demanded as self-righteous anger crashed into place. 'You used me and, believe me, you deserved every accusation I flung at you!'

'I knew you couldn't just come up here and talk! I knew sooner or later you would start again on the tired old gold-digger road!'

'You're having another man's baby! How do you think I feel? Do you think it's easy for me to sit here and tell you that I just don't give a damn *whose* baby you are carrying just so long as I am in the picture? Do you think I feel happy at finding myself in the position of needing to employ a private detective because I could not bear the thought of not knowing what was going on in your life?'

Lucy's mouth dropped open and she struggled to make sense of what he was telling her. What *was* he telling her? Surely not that *he loved her*? She could barely breathe.

'It's *your* baby,' was all she could find to say.

'That is impossible.' Nick's jaw hardened. Lord, but he wanted to move, except the kitchen was so restricting that his only option was to remain where he was, pinned into the chair by the woman staring at him and lying through her teeth.

'*How?* How is it *impossible*? We had sex. We weren't using protection at the time. Tell me why it's so impossible for me to get pregnant. Did your mother never tell you about the birds and the bees?'

Nick gritted his teeth together and inhaled deeply. 'It is impossible because I cannot father children.'

Lucy opened her mouth to speak but nothing emerged, while he continued to stare at her, his body absolutely still.

'You've had…had a vasectomy?'

Nick laughed harshly. 'A vasectomy? Me? I would never have a vasectomy. I have always wanted a family of my own!' He'd never thought that he would confess to anyone this secret that he had carried around with him for such a long time, and the feeling of being utterly and completely at someone else's mercy was so alien to him that he literally didn't know where to look or what next to say. But, lord, he adored this woman, and he would adore her child, even if it wasn't his, even if it had been conceived with all the wrong intentions. And she would love him back; he would teach her how.

'Then how do you know that you can't have children, Nick?'

'Because,' he said, sighing heavily and staring at the tips of his fingers, 'when I married Gina I wanted to start a family straight away, but nothing happened. Eventually she went to the doctor and was told that everything was fine with her. And I...well, I went too. I was told that I...I did not have what was necessary.'

'The doctor told you this?'

'Well, Gina went in to collect the letter and she reported it back to me. Very faithfully. She knew that there was no way that I would want to read it in black and white so she remembered precisely what was contained in it.'

'She lied.'

Nick's head shot up and he narrowed his eyes on her. 'What?'

'She lied,' Lucy said simply. 'Because I am carrying *your* baby, Nick, and that's all there is to it. Robert and I have never slept together.'

A thread of hope began to unfurl in the pit of his stomach and he fought against the temptation of being seduced by it.

'Of course, there's only one way of finding out the truth, if you're brave enough to do it, and that's to go back to the doctor and have another test done.' In the ensuing silence Lucy thought back to what else he had said and a slow smile curved her mouth. 'You mean you would have chosen to support me, even thinking that...the baby wasn't yours?'

Nick looked at her defiantly and his defiance took years away from his face. What she saw was an uncertain boy, holding his breath, daring to say things he would rather not have said, and her heart wanted to explode.

'Is it my fault that I fell in love with you?'

'You love me?'

'There you go again,' he muttered, and she took a few steps forward until she was close enough to touch him, and touch him she did, running trembling fingers through his dark, springy hair, tilting his face up to hers.

'Take the test, Nick. The baby is yours and I love you back.' The sob that had been trying to escape since she had spun around in the street an hour earlier and set eyes on him again finally found its way out. 'I think I was born to love you and I haven't stopped, even when you threw me out of your office and called me everything under the sun. I adore you and I don't want you to have any doubts that this is your baby.'

Easier said than done, he thought two days later as they waited for the doctor to stick his spectacles on and read the short letter he was holding. Lucy squeezed his hand and he squeezed hers back, albeit half-heartedly.

'Well,' Dr Thomas said, peering over the rims of his narrow reading glasses, 'this is as conclusive as anything you could hope for.'

'That I am…?'

'As fertile as any red-blooded man could hope to be. In fact, my boy, fertile enough for you to become a donor should you ever want to. I have no idea how you could have imagined that you couldn't have children.' He removed his spectacles and dangled them loosely from one hand. 'You could go ahead and have dozens.'

'Dozens!' Nick turned to Lucy the minute they were outside. 'Dozens! I can father dozens of children if I want!'

'Whoa!' She grinned at him and nestled into the crook of his arm, barely wanting to tear herself away to step into the taxi that whizzed them off to his apartment.

'What I don't understand,' she said thoughtfully as they walked into his sitting room, 'is why Gina would lie.' She knew all about their marriage, knew that she would never be living in the shadow of a woman he could not forget.

'Because it suited her to have this trump card to hold over me,' Nick said grimly. It was hard to feel angry, though, because he was so bloody happy. 'She relished being able to fall back on that final insult whenever there was an argument. She knew what my response would be, that I would walk out of the house because there was nothing to say when she accused me of being less of a man than she had hoped.' He went to sit by her and pulled her onto his lap so that her head was resting on the arm of the sofa and she was stretched out in front of him. Just the smallest of bumps proclaimed the baby growing inside her, and he rucked up her shirt so that he could place his hand there.

'I was crazy to believe her,' he said, 'and even crazier not to believe you when you told me about the pregnancy.'

'It was understandable. Suddenly you felt you could no longer trust me.'

'Yet I couldn't stop loving you. I couldn't turn that off like a tap.' He ran his hand up to caress her breast, which was fuller and heavier now, the nipple larger and darker and more prominent. He stroked the stiffened bud and smiled when she released a little sigh of pleasure.

'There's only one thing left for us to do,' he murmured, and Lucy looked drowsily at his dear face.

'Does it involve the bed?'

'That too. But, no, I was more thinking of marriage, and sooner rather than later.'

It was something she hadn't broached, knowing how he felt about that ultimate step after what he had been through, and her heart swelled at the love darkening his eyes when he looked at her.

'How soon, my darling?'

'As soon as possible?'

'I'll get on to it right now...'